Boomers
for the
Stars

SUE HOLLISTER BARR

ACKNOWLEDGMENTS

All artwork done by
Josue Ledesma.

SUE HOLLISTER BARR

"It's all I want!"

"Now, Mary, be a good little girl. You're not being sensible. Lands...girls don't even get to go to a city and get work when they grow up, except maybe to join a typing pool—if they can type—or even I helped some in the factories when the menfolk were all 'over there' fighting Hitler. Sakes alive, Mary! You want to go somewhere even men can't figure out how to get to?"

"It's all I'll ever want!"

"All you'll be wanting is the good sense to do what you're told and mind the people that take care of you. Start with me, your mama, and maybe, just maybe, when you grow up you'll be pretty enough to catch a good husband and do as he says, so he'll take care of you."

Mary stomped her feet in frustration till clouds of good Virginian topsoil billowed out around her.

Her mama tightened a tattered apron around the berries they'd gone out to pick in the middle of the night, because the menfolk had suddenly felt a hankering for berries. Mama looked up at the farmhouse.

Mary looked up at the stars.

"You can't do anything in this world unless you mind what others say, now. You can't do anything a'tall without the help of others, Mary. You'll see."

Mary heard her mama cross the porch and the slam of the screen door as she went inside. But Mary never took her eyes off the stars.

Draco, snaking its way through the northern skies. The gentle curve of Ursa Minor. The overbearing, bigger bear to her left. Mary knew all the constellations by heart.

The dust and the suffocating heat of the day settled beneath her bare feet. The song of the cicadas crescendoed. The night sky was crisp and clean and free.

Free from chores. Free from always having to say "yes'm" even when her heart screamed "no, ma'am." Free from having to hear her family tell "old colored man" jokes about the father of her only friend, before they lynched him.

Yes'm, she'd mind what others said. Yes'm, she'd always remember she had to rely on other people. But, no ma'am, she didn't care what her mama said about the only thing she'd ever want.

She'd find a way. Someday she'd get to the stars.

"'Boomers for the Stars.' Hidoi! What a dump."

The voice of a young woman Mary had never heard before. Strange accent. And what did "hidoi" mean? It was said as if the young woman had just stepped in a fresh cow patty or something equally icky. But, more importantly, where did this young woman's voice come from since Mary was all alone? Mary looked down, and for just a moment she saw wrinkles and liver spots on the backs of her own hands. And funny-looking soil she knew wasn't Virginia. And a funny-looking shoe belonging to someone standing behind her. Mary was confused. She was always confused now, and she hated being confused.

Then she got excited when she remembered. She loved it when she remembered things.

Stasis. Of course. It had been a long flight between stars. Explained her thinking she was still a little girl. Her perfect immersion in memories of Virginia. But actually she was Star Captain on a very dangerous mission and she had to—

"And who might you be?" That strange young woman's voice again.

Mary was confused again, but she turned and answered curtly, "I'm Mary, Star Captain."

"Uh huh... So how do they treat you here...Captain Mary?"

"You mean in my rocketship?"

"Uh, sure, yeah, in your rocketship. How do they treat the...uh...crew?"

Either an alien or a bot. Only explanation for all the speech hesitancy. Mary had to be careful. "Very well, thank you. And how do they treat you? On the planet Mongo."

"It keeps them happy, ne? Stop cringing." A young man speaking to the young woman with the same strange accent.

"But I can't stand the thought of Dad being in such a place. Extraordinary longevity's commonplace, ne? But, unlike most of the other Boomers, Dad's still lucid. Naïve, gullible, and hopelessly old-fashioned, perhaps, but lucid." The young woman again.

Something was going wrong with Mary now, some ripple in the time-space continuum. She could no longer see her rocketship! She figured it must be the work of the aliens, or bots, or whatever this young woman and young man really were.

Mary looked down, and for just a moment she saw grass, though scruffy and mostly crabgrass. Lots of litter, too. Closest to Mary was a hand-sized, rectangular screen—broken but showing a date in the future when the US population exceeded half a billion. Mary looked straight up. No stars, just a uniform, unnatural-looking haze. Didn't even resemble a normal night sky. But then she looked in front of her and saw them...

They were beautiful! Stars of every possible description: great red giants, teeny white dwarfs...and all so close to each other and easy to see! Mary figured she must be in heaven, not religiously but literally. Her childhood dream, all she had ever wanted, had come true. But then the young woman behind her stepped forward and passed a hand through a red giant that made it jump and stutter a bit before re-forming. Mary looked above all the stars and was startled to see a sign:

BOOMERS FOR THE STARS
Technology keeping your loved ones alive forever?
We'll take them off your hands and send them to the stars.

Mary didn't know what any of that meant. Or how a sign could be floating around in space, so big that it spread across all the stars. Or how a person's hand could be as big as a red giant star and pass right through it. Mary was very confused again. But she knew her crew was depending on her. She looked back at all the stars. She searched and searched among them. Where was her rocketship? And how could she be floating around among the stars without a space suit?

SUE HOLLISTER BARR

Colonel Jethro Hayes watched his kids come in with "Star Captain Mary." Poor old broad. Really shouldn't be allowed to spend half the night on the front lawn, staring at their nursing home's elaborately holographed sign. Jethro would have to speak to that boy he'd spotted about it. But of course staying inside meant she'd have "JFK," "Marilyn Monroe," and "Napoleon" around to confuse her.

For himself, Jethro was rather partial to "Napoleon." Might only be guessing when you asked him what century they were living in now, but the man knew his military history...at least up until the early 19th century. They could talk strategy forever, all of it from long before

SmartSoldiers with their SmartWeapons. All of it harkening back to a time when men were men and fought with their own wits, not some AI-induced automated strategy.

They were just debating Prussian configurations at Waterloo—while a bot that looked like a grotesquely oversized rubber ducky was scanning his kids' retinas before admitting them—when "Marilyn Monroe" interrupted.

"Where's Jack?" she breathed.

As in Kennedy. Didn't look any more like JFK than this shriveled old broad looked like Marilyn Monroe, of course, but he did a damn fine job of delivering the "ask not what your country can do for you" speech.

"Napoleon" preened, then fussed over finding just the right pose. "Jacques-Louis David?"

Jethro remembered the famous portrait of the real Napoleon. "Different Jack. Not the painter." He turned to "Marilyn," who was batting her nonexistent eyelashes. "Jack went in for prep this morning." Then Jethro puffed out his chest and added, because he couldn't resist with his kids approaching, "I'm next!"

"Next for what, Dad?" asked his daughter.

"Next Boomer for the Stars, of course!"

His daughter should have beamed. Instead she and his son glanced at his wheelchair before exchanging a look. Why? Wasn't he going to the stars anyway? He wasn't like these others with bodies kept alive long after their minds were gone. He, Colonel Jethro Hayes, would be an truly invaluable asset to any expedition in search of humanity's new home!

"Why the look, my darling daughter?"

"Nothing, Dad, nothing."

"At heart, you're as curious as a cat. Why aren't you curious to know about what will be my last, no-return mission?" Something in her eyes made him anxious. Leaning toward her, he knocked over "Napoleon's" brandy snifter by mistake.

"At heart, you're as clumsy as a pig," his daughter threw back with a wink.

Jethro put his hand to his chest. No scar of course. Long time ago. But he still remembered coming out from under the anesthesia with a distinct craving to roll in some mud. And he'd seen the dead pig on his doctor bot's full-disclosure screen. "Can't argue with you there..."

The rubber-ducky bot sucked up the mess, replacing the snifter before "Napoleon" noticed. Over its full-disclosure screen, currently reviewing brands of brandy before selecting one for "Napoleon," Jethro spotted that boy again.

"You there!" he called out. "You, boy, over here!"

No response. Too dumb to know he was being called most likely.

"Boy! Over here!"

"Dad, who are you calling boy?"

"Why that colored man over there."

She turned. At the sight of the boy she giggled a bit, blushed, and blurted out, "Sugoi!"

"Not that Jap slang again. You know I hate it when..."

The boy looked up quickly, gave her a look no colored man should ever give a white woman, and grinned. Jethro missed his old army-issued M-16 from Nam, whether it jammed or not.

"Eeee, Dad, that young man isn't black."

"Well he certainly isn't white!"

"Dad, how many times do I have to explain, no one's white anymore...or black. We're all mixed up, and none of that old archaic nonsense matters anymore. You're embarrassing me!" Then she called out to the boy, "Ne, ne, what's your name?"

"Brooklyn," said the boy, and he spun around toward her, showing off, and knocked over "Napoleon's" brandy snifter again. "Wasup, B? Smile like that once more, fair maiden, and I'll stab thee in thine own house."

Jethro almost bolted out of his wheelchair on that one, but his daughter pushed him back.

"Not stab with a knife, Dad. It's Shakespeare. Very sugoi."

Jethro frowned.

"Very cool," his daughter translated.

Jethro was seething. "Where's your brother?"

"We have to thumbprint some screens before you're completely official in your new home here. I have to thumbprint, too. I'll be back."

She took off, and Jethro watched her walking through the cheesy holography that pretended to be what was once called a shag carpet. But the color kept changing, and the programming that was supposed to make it appear to depress with her footsteps was out of sync, so she appeared to be following an invisible doppelganger. The wallpaper was even worse, a tacky idea to begin with, lined with old masters' portraits that were supposed to follow a person walking by with their eyes. Instead the eyes just turned to what reminded Jethro of old television static every time someone walked by.

He felt a hand on his shoulder. "Wasup, B?" It was that colored boy. Mighty uppity.

"Don't you have more sense than to lay your hands on a white man?"

"A what man? Oh...you. You are very pale. Why? Is it contagious?"

"Race isn't contagious, you fool!"

"Race? Eeee, your accent. Is that southern U.S.?"

"Marilyn" pushed between them. "Jack! Oh, Jack!" Jethro stared at her in disbelief. Marilyn Monroe's speech and mannerisms were gone. An occupant of this body he'd never seen stood gasping, hand to her mouth. "Oh, no, how can this be?" She seemed rather elegant. But Jethro forgot all about that when she pushed through and kneeled on the floor, confusing the shag-carpet holography into a frenzy of color changes, calling "Jack" over and over again, and blocking Jethro's view.

A pink-panda bot from the lab was sucking a trail of something up off the floor that Jethro couldn't quite see through the shag-carpet holography. Finally he remembered the out-of-sync footprint programming and looked just ahead of the pink-panda bot, where it hadn't sucked whatever it was up yet. Sure enough, the out-of-sync programming depressed the carpet before Pink Panda's wheels got there, and Jethro could see what it was.

Blood. Damn. Jethro knew prepping for a mission could be brutal, especially one as important as finding humanity's new home, light years away. But that was a whole shit-load of blood "Jack" had lost.

The boy ran after "Marilyn," stumbling. It was the kind of stumble that gave away what must be AI-powered leg supports for someone who would otherwise be in a wheelchair. Jethro took a moment to snarl at the thought of all the bleeding-heart liberals that had probably mandated that a nursing home hire the handicapped. Then he saw "Marilyn," who'd been blocking his view, collapse in tears, and got his first view of "Jack."

He still managed, somehow, to look like JFK, even though he was sprawled across the floor, completely confusing the shag-carpet programming's color stability. He must have crawled out of the prep rooms, but Jethro couldn't figure out how, given the extent of his wounds. His injuries were surgically done, completely lacking the jagged edges and random quality of everything Jethro had seen in Nam. And lethal. It only took an old soldier like Jethro a glance to see that.

"JFK's" eyes had been removed, but he miraculously managed to open his mouth. "Victory has a thousand fathers," he sputtered through a fountain of blood. He coughed up some kind of surgical device before finishing, "but defeat is an orphan." Something else must have been left in his throat; he started to choke. Feebly he reached up with one hand, as high as he could reach.

Pink Panda's full-disclosure screen flashed a floorplan of the nursing home. Blinking red dots seemed to indicate outsiders, like the two that were probably Jethro's kids in the administrative offices. The bot seemed to be doing something to all the doors that separated red-dotted outsiders from where "JFK" lay, probably locking them.

"JFK" waved his shaking hand around wildly, grasping at air.

The boy cradled "JFK" very gently, fingers in his mouth but apparently failing to reach the obstruction.

"Star Captain Mary" made photon torpedo sounds.

"Napoleon" shook his head.

"Marilyn" sobbed.

Pink Panda reached out for "JFK's" outstretched hand, just as he stretched it so high it seemed he was determined to reach the stars after all, and cut it off. The stump was a fountain of red the bot quickly cauterized, while its full-disclosure screen scrolled through what seemed to be a black-market price list for human body parts, sorted by price, and cut into "JFK's" knee. Blood splattered over its shiny pink fur.

The dayroom's rubber-ducky bot approached with what Jethro recognized were medication injections. Jethro, who had seen a lot in his life, realized he was about to faint.

SUE HOLLISTER BARR

Kane thought his new job was so sugoi. He grinned. Boomers for the Stars might not look like much but—yabai!—he was sure he could turn it into a great nursing home. The bots were good. It was just that they'd been left without human direction for too long and needed a little remedial work.

That brother and sister thumbprinting screens in his director's office were cute, especially the sister. "Almost done so we can talk, ne?"

The brother grabbed at a screen floating in the air between them. "Before I thumbprint this one, what's this about agreeing to remove all Dad's personal belongings now that he's settled in?"

"His actual personal belongings are no longer necessary," Kane explained. "Holography's now programmed to duplicate them all. And projections are much safer since you know how older loved ones can forget where things are or, much worse, fall on them and hurt themselves."

"Same software that controls the carpeting?"

"Touché," Kane conceded. "So hidoi." He wrinkled his nose in disgust, then brightened. "But that carpeting is a good example of how we cut costs in non-essential areas. For family members like you, saving all the money you can without compromising your father's physical well-being and happiness is important, ne?"

The brother paused, fidgeting with the thumb he hadn't yet applied to that screen. Kane, knowing all their father's possessions were already packed up and waiting inside the patient dayroom, held his breath. Left in the dayroom too long, anything could happen. Someone might even stow away in all that junk and escape. Finally the brother thumbed it and moved on.

Now the sister looked up and smiled.

Kane thought he was in love.

"What about this fine print about how when you check into a nursing home you give up your right not to be experimented on?" she asked.

This was a subject Kane was prepared to put his heart into...still original equipment, 100% human, in his case. "One of those hidoi global directives. Can't get rid of it; you'll never find a nursing home without it. But of course there isn't a nursing home still in business today that experiments on its patients!" He winked at her and smiled back. Yabai, she was cute!

She frowned at her screen, still uncertain and looking all the more adorable for it, but she finally thumbed it.

They talked. Kane even got misty-eyed when he described his determination to make Boomers for the Stars the best it could be.

The sister looked interested.

Everything was beautiful.

She furrowed her brow.

Still very cute.

Then she suddenly looked like she was going to cry.

Kane would have more than welcomed the opportunity to wrap a comforting arm around her.

"What about..."

This was clearly hard for her.

"...the stars?"

"Definitely part of our program," Kane assured her.

"I...wasn't sure anyone was still sending Boomers to the stars."

"Sure they are. It's just not all over the news the way it was when this nursing home was named. But here—especially here, with this name—we have a proud tradition to maintain!"

"But...the treatments to prep them...that's not something you'd invest in...in the case of... I mean he's completely lucid, not like all those Boomers who think they're someone famous or that poor woman who thinks she's already in the stars, but... That horrible accident! You wouldn't invest in preparing someone in a wheelchair for the stars!"

"Have faith in us, in me! We perform miracles around here!"

That slow, hopeful smile. Kane would have said anything to earn that. Finally, after a few easier questions, they got up and left.

Kane knew he'd just have to find a reason to call her really soon, something about her dad, anything.

The lab's pink-panda bot wheeled in, its full-disclosure screen showing that it, too, was thinking about—and tracking—the daughter's departure.

"Patient termination," it vocalized.

"Who?" asked Kane.

"Donald Johnson."

"Who?"

"'JFK.'"

"Ah. What did you get?"

The pink panda presented its screen.

Kane looked it over. "What about the kidneys?"

"Damaged in the process of dying."

Kane sprang to his feet. "You waited until he was dying to harvest parts? You let parts as valuable as the kidneys get damaged?" Kane was beside himself. These bots were going to need a lot more than a little remedial work.

Star Captain Mary was cramped,
but it was unavoidable. She'd had to hide
in one of her rocketship's teeny cargo
bays to escape that pink furry alien she'd
seen murder one of her own dear crew
members, no matter how many times she
blasted it with her secret death ray. She
also had to fight back tears. That alien
cutting the hand off that her dear crew
member had stretched out while choking
had been so very dreadful.

She was being jostled about now, along with the cargo, but she didn't care. She had to get help! She had to save the rest of her crew!

Suddenly all the jostling stopped. Mary heard a clanging, ridiculously loud mechanical announcement: "Authentic Archibald A. Astor's..." There was a slight pause. "...best liquid cart tune-up on Earth. Guaranteed you'll only need to buy half the hydrogen afterwards or your money back."

Then Mary heard human voices. Those same two voices she'd first heard when she found that weird, gigantic sign about "Boomers for the Stars" floating around in space.

"Shimatta!" the young woman snapped in annoyance. "An old sales bot standing right in the middle of the road, ne? And with a two-dimensional sign." The young woman went on, but softer and slower now. "What are we going to do with all Dad's personal belongings?"

"You're not going to like this..." It was the young man.

"Like what? Start up the cart again. I want to get home."

Mary shifted carefully. It felt like she was encased in a mattress.

The man sighed. "If you want to get home again, it makes no sense to squander all our hydrogen hauling around Dad's bedroom furniture."

"But I thought we agreed that the nursing home was only temporary."

Silence.

The woman again. "You... You never meant it to be temporary!"

"No," he answered, "I didn't. So hidoi... But think about it. There's barely enough room left in this poor, super-industrialized Africa for the two of us, let alone Dad and all his junk. If we bring Dad back home, we'll never save enough money to leave the third world and go somewhere civilized enough that they no longer have cities."

"But to leave poor Dad in Africa, in such a place—"

"Paid for by grant funding? Where he'll probably eat better than we can afford to?"

Her turn to sigh. "His roll-top desk from the 19th century? In better shape after over two hundred years than he is, even though he's a little younger? All that southern-U.S. memorabilia from his 1950s childhood?"

"In one of our super-cramped African cubicles after we sell his apartment?"

Silence again.

Then some crying, his. "I know, I know! Shimatta, I hate to do it!"

A door hissed open. Mary could hear some moving around, then the woman's voice from farther away. "Come on. If it has to be done, let's get to it."

After that there were a lot of doors hissing open, along with tilts that sent Mary sliding from one end of her mattress cocoon to the other. Finally there was a rough jolt, a hard landing, and fresh air.

The man was crying again.

Mary stayed hidden in the folded mattress, but there was some rustling around close to her head.

The woman's voice, very close to Mary, was soft. "Here."

The man was having trouble talking between his sobs. "What's...what's that?"

"Dad's Confederate flag. I think he'd want you to have it, ne? Remember him as the son of the Confederacy he was so proud of being—even if he was born a century too late to fight in the Civil War."

"In my cubicle there's not enough room for an extra folded napkin—"

"Unfold his flag and use it like wallpaper behind the shelves. You'll still be able to stretch your legs out almost straight, on the diagonal of course, when you sleep, ne?"

Now they were both crying, but all the sounds were getting softer, farther away. Until Mary heard that mechanical announcement again: "Authentic Archibald A. Astor's..." There was another pause. "...best liquid anti-depressant on Earth. Guaranteed you'll never cry again, even if you live to be 250, or your money back."

Then doors hissed again, and Mary heard what she suddenly remembered was the sound of a hydrogen cart starting up back on Earth.

Star Captain Mary was confused again, but she waited until she couldn't hear the hydrogen cart anymore. Then she poked her head out from the mattress before crawling out and standing. At which point she was even more confused.

It looked like she was on an Earth-sized planet, covered with towering, crumbling buildings. As far as she could see, horizon to horizon in all directions, any land that was left over served as an infinite, open dump, piled high with refuse that now included her mattress cocoon, which turned out to be two mattresses, one on top of the other.

The only exception was a skinny, single-lane road. But, like drifting snow, the garbage even encroached on that. Otherwise the road was empty, apart from what looked like a half-disassembled bot holding an old-fashioned, two-dimensional sign projector and staring at Mary. She was wondering why it was staring at her when movement registered in her peripheral vision, and she returned her attention to the refuse.

The garbage was moving, undulating gently and rhythmically. It was then that Mary realized there were people who appeared to be living in it.

One was tugging at one of her mattresses. "Finders keepers!"

"Where's my rocketship?"

Except for the half-disassembled bot, the whole garbage dump seemed to break into laughter.

"'Rocketship'?" came a voice behind her. "Flash Gordon, ne? Didn't think anyone was into super retro 'sci fi' anymore."

The one tugging at a mattress yanked it free. Something that must have been stuck between the two mattresses fell out, landing near Mary's feet.

"'Rocketship'?" came from farther away. "Plenty of room for one over here. Wait a minute. Yup. Sugoi! I see it. Come help me dig it out."

46

There was another flurry of laughter.

Someone was looking at the roll-top desk. Another picked up a toy Dukes-of-Hazzard car with one hand and a book about the Civil War with the other.

Mary picked up whatever had fallen out from between the two mattresses, which turned out to be a cracked leather Aunt Jemima purse. She peeked inside; there was money.

A new voice called out. "Maybe you can sell that 'rocketship' for the seven thousand it would cost you to get back to New York Un-City."

Chuckles rippled through the crowd, with an occasional, bitter, "I wish!"

Mary was still confused, but she was pretty sure she'd always been good at math. She hunkered down behind the remaining mattress and counted the money in the Aunt Jemima purse. Eight thousand.

Then she straightened up and headed toward the person who'd found her rocketship. But this was greeted by a blizzard of guffaws. Dimly, slowly, looking into the faces of the people she passed, Mary realized she was the source of seemingly infinite hilarity.

"If only this poor, demented Boomer could get back to the U.S. for some elder mind care."

"I remember the last super retro 'sci fi' craze. First she has to save the planet Earth by getting to the planet Mongo."

Mary stumbled over what appeared to be some of the half-disassembled bot's missing pieces. Someone had used them to make a crude stove. She tried to get up but fell back down again to a chorus of giggles.

Her leg was bleeding, and her shin bone hurt horribly, but she had to get to her rocketship. She had to save the rest of her crew. Putting a hand down for support, her palm was cut on something. Her other hand landed on garbage that shifted beneath her, spilling her over sideways.

Finally she managed to stand. Wasn't there anyone on this horrible planet who would help? Turning full circle, looking into each face, all she saw was laughter. "Someone help me!" she called out. "I'm confused! But I have to get back to my rocketship!"

The laughter was so loud it almost drowned out the clanging mechanical announcement: "Authentic Archibald A. Astor's..." Pause. "...best liquid elderly tune-up on Earth. Guaranteed you'll never feel confused again, even if you live till 250, or your money back."

Mary turned. The bot was right next to her. Beside it was the man who had taken one of Mary's mattresses. He glared at the bot and rolled his eyes.

Mary was torn. She looked toward where that other dump-dweller had said her rocketship was. She looked toward the half-disassembled bot that had just promised she'd never be confused again. Mary hated being confused all the time.

"Oh, no!" It was the mattress man. Mary looked away from the bot for a moment and saw him watching her, wide-eyed. "You're not seriously..." He looked at the bot next to him and doubled over laughing.

Mary didn't understand. If she was confused, how could she help her crew when evil aliens might be cutting their hands off at this very moment, and even her secret death ray hadn't saved the last one. She approached the bot. "How much money will it cost to guarantee that I'm never confused again?" She held out the Aunt Jemima purse.

"That will be a hundred," started the bot.

Mattress Man snatched the purse out of her hand. "I can put that to a lot better use than anyone so dumb she—" He interrupted himself when he looked inside, counting quickly. "Why there's eight thousand here."

"That will be eight thousand," corrected the bot.

Suddenly the man who'd taken the mattress looked sad and said, speaking to no one in particular, "I'm going to hate myself for this." He took a thousand out of the purse, zipped it up, and held both the thousand and the purse out toward Mary. "Listen to me very carefully and do exactly what I say: Take this thousand and hide it in your clothes. Take this purse and hide it in a different place in your clothes. Don't talk to anybody, don't even say a word out loud, but follow this road to the port." He pointed down the road.

Mary took the purse and the thousand.

"Right next to all the desalination plants and the space elevator is an airpad. Look for an orange bot that has 'Tickets Here' floating above it. Only then do you bring out the purse. Understand?"

Mary nodded.

"Tell the bot you want a ticket to anywhere in the U.S. that you can get to for seven thousand. The bot will understand. It's what all of us want, all of us who were so stupid that we came here when all the people who were living here originally were smart enough to get out."

Mary felt her brow wrinkle in confusion.

"Never mind all that, just tell the bot that all you have is seven thousand, and you're willing to go anywhere in the United States. Once you get to the U.S., go to the nearest hospital... You got that? Go to the nearest hospital?"

Again, Mary nodded.

"Go to the nearest hospital and tell them you're willing to be a subject for their elder mind care experiments. Repeat what I just said."

"Elder mind care experiments."

Then Mattress Man did something really strange, so strange that his face kind of shuddered through it, like he'd forgotten how to do it: he smiled. "Okay, I'm out of here. Before I come to my senses and take that money back, ne?" He did an about-face and marched off, bobbing up and down over the garbage.

Mary watched him go. "Go down the road that way," she whispered to herself. "Airpad at the port. Go to the United States." But was she remembering it right? She remembered she wasn't supposed to speak out loud, but it burst out of her in a scream: "I'm so confused!"

Mary heard the clanging, ridiculously loud mechanical announcement behind her: "Authentic Archibald A. Astor's..." There was a slight pause. "...best liquid elderly tune-up on Earth. Guaranteed you'll never feel confused again, even if you live till 250, or your money back."

She turned.

The bot had its money receiver extended. "That will be eight thousand."

Mary was still holding the thousand and the purse.

There was laughter behind her and, somewhere, her rocketship, where her crew needed her to be clear-headed.

Mary gave the bot the money.

The bot gave her a dirty looking vial.

"Where'd you get that?" asked someone behind her.

The clanging, mechanical answer was, "Fell off a cart." It pointed in the opposite direction, away from the port. "A cart going that way."

Mary looked at the vial. It said something about it having been made in the U.S. and that it was only for purposes of research. And the name Archibald A. Astor. She snapped the lid off and drank it.

The laughter died abruptly. Mary turned to see that all the laughing faces had changed to expressions of horror, especially Mattress Man, who seemed to

have frozen in the act of running back
toward her.

But why had all these people been
laughing at a Star Captain anyway?
Mary looked out at the earth-like planet
she was on. That stuff she drank...it was
making her sick. She started spitting up all
kinds of weird stuff that didn't seem to be
food. She caught sight of the backs of
her hands, but...was it her imagination or
did she see wrinkles and liver spots that
were fading? Her head felt funny. Maybe
all these people had been laughing
because she wasn't really a Star Captain.

Colonel Jethro Hayes didn't understand why he was fixated on such a minor matter, but he kept thinking about how the thing he missed the most was his toy Dukes-of-Hazzard car. A memory of their nursing home's JFK reaching for the stars and getting his hand cut off intruded but was buried immediately beneath bitterness over being told that his kids had taken all his stuff. Angry. That's what he was, he told himself. The news that Star Captain Mary had disappeared added to it. Poor old broad should never have been left out on the lawn staring at the Boomers sign. Not with all those live-forever lion clones that had escaped from all those pre-industrial amusement parks.

The unmistakable scent of Chanel No. 5 tickled Jethro's nose.

"Where's Jack?" Marilyn breathed.

"Still in prep," Jethro lied, irrationally annoyed by the innocence in her eyes, but proud that he was still enough of a southern gentleman to do what was necessary where a lady was concerned.

When Jethro fainted after watching JFK die, the bots might have thought he'd slept through the whole thing. Apparently they hadn't bothered to inject him. But they must have injected everyone else with what they used to call "fuhgeddaboudit," because not one of the other patients remembered what had happened to JFK.

A warm hand squeezed Jethro's shoulder. "Wasup, B?"

It was that uppity colored boy who should have been in a wheelchair, not paid to work at a nursing home so he could let lion clones eat its patients. Jethro shook his shoulder free. "Unhand me!"

"Say what?"

"You heard me, boy. Think those fancy leg braces fool me? You should be in a wheelchair."

"Like you?"

Jethro didn't understand what that fool boy was talking about until he finally looked down at his own wheelchair. That was another thing Jethro didn't allow himself to think about. Like that image Jethro was trying to push out of his mind...of this boy cradling JFK, trying to save his life by finding the obstruction in his throat. Doing something he, Jethro, hadn't been able to do.

"Hidoi..." the boy said softly and sadly, staring at Jethro as if horrified by Jethro's hideous condition.

Jethro hated Jap slang. And it reminded him of the flirty conversation this colored boy had had with Jethro's own daughter.

Boy had the effrontery to lean over to pat, then rub, Jethro's back. "I get it, B. I started out in a wheelchair myself—"

Despite the difference in their ages and Jethro's wheelchair, Jethro spun on that boy and managed to connect with a right upper cut.

Despite the boy's fancy leg braces, he lost his balance and sprawled on the floor, rubbing his chin and completely confusing the shag-carpet programming. "Shimatta!" he cursed, but with what looked like grudging respect. "You pack a wallop."

Jethro rolled over the boy's outstretched hand with his wheelchair.

Marilyn gasped.

The boy's admiration vanished, contempt accompanying his angry curses now. "Kuso, jiji, pluck off!"

"You think this wheelchair's going to stop me from getting prepped for the stars?" Jethro couldn't believe the words coming out of his mouth. Like JFK was "prepped"? But some demon forced him to push on. "You work here, boy, and all you can do is feed helpless old women to the lion clones."

Chanel No. 5. Close. Marilyn was helping the boy up, frowning at Jethro. "His name is Brooklyn. And he doesn't work here. He's a patient, just like you.

Young, but crippled. Me?" She struck a classic Marilyn Monroe pose with half-closed eyes. "I'm a movie star."

Two bots wheeled into the dayroom.

Jethro stiffened, all thoughts of his missing Dukes-of-Hazzard car and this colored boy named "Brooklyn" gone. His poor pig heart froze with fear as he realized, too late, that the only thing he should have been concerning himself with was why his kids hadn't returned his urgent calls.

The bots were dragging someone unconscious between them. Someone covered with filth and vomit. The head flopped back; it was Star Captain Mary! For a fraction of a second Jethro was relieved that she'd been found alive. Then he looked at the bots, remembered JFK, and was horrified that she'd been found alive.

Kane, the new human director, rushed in after them.

Star Captain Mary started choking like JFK but—oddly, through all of it—somehow looked better, younger, more beautiful to Jethro than she'd ever looked. Then she vomited, the ultimate challenge for the shag-carpet programming, and her eyes snapped open. Was it Jethro's imagination or was Star Captain Mary, like Marilyn when she saw JFK die, no longer Star Captain Mary? She gave her surroundings a quick look and Jethro thought he saw the same fear in her eyes that he felt in his pig heart. Had she, like Jethro, somehow escaped the bots' injections after the JFK incident? But, even if she had, the bigger miracle would be if she actually understood what was happening around her.

Kane, the new human nursing home director... Jethro thought about him. Slick. Polished. The "modern man." Again, was it Jethro's imagination or did Kane look angry at the bots for bringing Star Captain Mary in? Jethro couldn't understand him, so he couldn't risk trusting him.

But Kane certainly didn't sound angry at anyone or anything when he smiled around at all the patients in the dayroom and started to talk. "All of us here, staff and patients, are family. We're not perfect. Our leaving Star Captain Mary outside for so long was obviously a mistake; she must have caught some horrible bug. But we have to stick together."

Marilyn stuck her chest out and approached him. "Where's Jack?"

Kane puffed up like a proud father. "On his way to Alpha Centauri."

Napoleon clapped. Everyone, except Star Captain Mary, looked happy.

Jethro's pig heart sank as his suspicions about Kane were confirmed.

Kane approached the bots, manually typing something into their full-disclosure screens with an urgency that was at odds with his otherwise relaxed manner. Then he addressed the patients again. "Star Captain Mary?"

"I'm not a—"

"Yours is the honor of being the next Boomer we're going to prep for the stars."

Jethro could have sworn her eyes widened in fear, but then she smiled and clapped her hands together in glee, poor thing. "Star Captain Mary reporting for duty!" Miraculously, she stood up straight. "Permission requested to retrieve my spaceship from the front lawn first." She was already headed toward the door.

She might have made it, but Marilyn and that colored boy Brooklyn got in her way, congratulating her, and then Kane caught up with her.

More than any southern gentleman could possibly endure. Jethro called out, "Wait a minute, Kane," while struggling to close the distance between them with his wheelchair.

Kane turned, wreathed with smiles. "Ah, Colonel! Before she goes you'd like to congratulate our beloved Star Captain—"

"Take me instead!" Jethro couldn't believe he got the words out of his mouth.

Kane, suddenly frowning, appeared to be having similar difficulties.

"It's not fair!" Jethro tucked his hands under his thighs, hoping Kane hadn't spotted how much they were shaking. "And it makes no sense."

Kane eyed him warily.

Jethro faked a light laugh. "Who's going to believe you aren't just harvesting body parts here if you take a psychotic woman covered with her own vomit before you take a twice-decorated colonel?"

Marilyn frowned. That boy Brooklyn looked downright hostile. Star Captain Mary looked confused, but that was business as usual for her.

Jethro kept at it. "Kane, if you're sending us Boomers to the stars, I—of those of us who remain—am your only logical next choice."

Brooklyn all but spat at Jethro, "Shimatta, jiji, away you three-inch fool!"

Kane studied the still-confused-looking Star Captain Mary.

Brooklyn took a step toward Jethro but tripped from what looked like a bent leg brace.

Kane, watching, fingered one of the bots' full-disclosure screens. Jethro was close enough now to see Kane scroll through something about the astronomical price of repairing and maintaining leg braces.

"Kane," said Brooklyn, "take Star Captain Mary now; you said you would, ne? But next time...yabai!...why take a violent jiji full of hate in a wheelchair, why take any Boomer, when you've got me?"

Full of hate? Fool! But Jethro had to concede that "violent" wasn't unjustified, coming from the one whose leg brace Jethro probably bent by knocking him down.

Kane darted looks between Brooklyn and Star Captain Mary before turning his back on them to address the rest of the patients. "Like I said before, we're all family here, all in this together. And, in a family, everyone has a say, and everyone's opinion is taken into consideration."

Star Captain Mary gave Brooklyn a look of deep sorrow, all signs of confusion gone.

Kane went on. "Our distinguished colonel does have some valid points about why Mary may not be...ready...just yet." He turned to Brooklyn, while fingering a bot's full-disclosure screen. "And you,

Brooklyn, have some valid points about why you should be next."

Both bots wheeled over to Brooklyn.

"Flexibility, adaptability and a willingness to change are everything. Everyone, please congratulate Brooklyn, our next..." Kane paused to smile and wink, "...not-a-Boomer for the stars."

Star Captain Mary was saved and so was he! Relief washed over Jethro, even a smirk over that uppity Brooklyn taking their places, until Jethro was sure he saw horrified pity in Star Captain Mary's eyes. She was still looking at Brooklyn.

And then it came back and wouldn't be silenced, suppressed, or buried: Jethro relived the full memory of what had happened to JFK, complete with Brooklyn cradling JFK gently and trying so hard to save him. Now Brooklyn was smiling as he faced a similar fate, because the bots had injected him with fuhgeddaboudit, and he didn't remember any of it.

Jethro had seen enough. He hadn't made colonel in Nam by standing by while others got their eyes cut out and their hands cut off.

"No, Kane," he heard himself say. "This no-account boy before a twice-decorated colonel?" Jethro looked deep into Kane's eyes, mustering all the authority he'd once wielded. "I can't imagine a regulatory board that would let that one slip by."

SUE HOLLISTER BARR

Kane, alone for a moment in his office, kicked a wall panel that annoyed him further by immediately repairing itself.

Shimatta! Stupid bots! Bringing a patient in Mary's condition into the dayroom for all the other patients to see? Almost as bad as letting JFK escape from the lab, though Kane had to acknowledge that JFK shouldn't have had anywhere near the strength to do that at his stage of organ harvesting.

Kane was still scratching his head over JFK and how he'd managed that. But, again, the real issue was the stupid bots. So hidoi. First, they'd made it impossible to collect payment for either experiment by combining two when even the stupidest human would have known conducting two experiments at the same time on the same subject invalidated both experiments. Then the first experiment, though it made JFK puke a lot, not only didn't kill him but seemed to make him stronger. And when the second experiment did kill him—as most of their typically illegal, black-market experiments did—the stupid bots hadn't harvested his kidneys in time.

Human judgment, it all came down to human judgment. Like exposing the other patients to Mary's condition so soon after they witnessed JFK's final moments. Eeee... Bots couldn't be expected to think beyond, "we'll just inject the witnesses again so they'll forget." Bots weren't haunted by the nursing-home scandals that meant all their family members would be grilling them about daily events, looking for holes in their memories.

Kane stared at the safe till it recognized his retinas and opened. He started foraging through client lab requests, a chaos of poorly packaged injectables from mad-scientist hobbyists who loved to experiment. Big pharma, assuming they even cared how their products affected human beings, would never do business with a place as shabby as Boomers for the Stars.

May as well get that first stupid-bot-invalidated experiment on JFK repeated, Kane thought, so he could get paid this time. He found the right package for the stuff that had make JFK puke and swiped aside the lab request to get to the vials. But he did note that, even accounting for the one used on JFK, they were still a few short of the number the lab request said was included.

Typical mad scientist, thought Kane. So convinced his brilliant invention will save the world that he's willing to pay his life savings for human experimentation, but he can't accurately count the number of vials he sends.

Kane grabbed a vial, waited for the safe to note he'd done so and confirm it was locked again, and bolted through the door of his office into the hall. He all but collided with the colonel and caught a look on his face that made Kane wonder if the bots had even bothered to inject the colonel after the JFK incident. It was not the look of someone who thought he'd soon be young again, having fun exploring the stars.

Hmmm, thought Kane. Might confirm his decision in the end to take the colonel out next. Sugoi... Sweet as sugar. Kane almost smiled.

But then he spotted the one he knew had escaped before getting an injection, the one he'd originally wanted to take out next. Until he'd decided she was still so already-in-the-stars out-of-it that her escape couldn't have been rational. "Star Captain Mary! To what do we owe the pleasure of your presence in the 'staff and star-preps only' section?"

Did the security doors here work as well as the shag carpeting?

Still covered with vomit, Mary snapped to attention. "Star Captain Mary reporting for duty!"

Of course, thought Kane. Couldn't expect her to remember he'd changed his mind and was taking the colonel next instead of her.

The bots had arrived with the colonel at the extra security door for the lab.

With a speed Kane wouldn't have believed possible, Star Captain Mary grabbed the controls for the colonel's wheelchair and headed back the other way, toward the exit into the dayroom. "Star Captain Mary requests permission to show the new recruit the rocketship first. Then I'll bring him right back to get prepped."

Kane stood between her and the door out of the staff area that lead back into the dayroom, but she went to push the colonel's wheelchair past Kane with a strength Kane didn't think was possible

"No, no, fair lady," the colonel protested, siding with Kane against her.

Shimatta! What a mess, Kane thought. But then Mary spotted the vial still in Kane's hand and—oddly, suddenly—let go of the colonel's wheelchair, backing through the exit and out of the staff-only area herself. "As you wish," she said to the colonel, "fair sir."

"It's all I want!"

"Now, Mary, be a good little girl. You're not being sensible..."

This time Mary envisioned herself sitting on the ground, that good Virginian topsoil, while she looked up at the stars. Draco, snaking its way through the northern skies. The gentle curve of Ursa Minor. The overbearing, bigger bear to her left. She knew all the constellations by heart.

Her mama's mantra again. "You can't do anything in this world unless you mind what others say. You can't do anything without the help of others, Mary."

But the night sky was crisp and clean and free. "It's all I'll ever want!"

High-heel footprints formed in the carpet Mary was sitting on first. Next came that perfume, whatever it was. Then a shriveled old woman with wisps of bleached-blonde hair. "Did you see Jack?"

Mary was confused and didn't know how to answer.

Marilyn clattered some rhinestone bracelets together, pointing at the staff-and-star-preps-only door next to Mary. "I saw you come out from there, Star Captain Mary, from where they took Jack. Is that how you get to Alpha Centauri?"

Mary wasn't confused anymore, and she knew just how to answer. "That's right! That's where they keep the rocketships! I just got back from Alpha Centauri. Jack is doing fine."

First his boot footprints, and then Napoleon joined them. "What's your strategy, Star Captain Mary?"

"Simple," said Mary, amazingly comfortable on the floor for someone as old as she was. Still, she winced when bot wheels appeared in the carpet, coming from the other side of the dayroom. But when the rubber-ducky bot arrived, it only cleaned the vomit off her. Mary continued to Napoleon, "However, we have to wait for the colonel first. He..." She brushed a bot sponge attachment aside to look at Marilyn. "...and Jack, of course, are surveying the situation. I'm waiting here for their report."

The pink-panda bot came through the staff-and-star-preps-only door next to Mary, scattering the crowd just as Brooklyn arrived.

Mary leaped to her feet. "The report I've been waiting for!"

Pink Panda angled its full-disclosure screen at them. It said something about how the human director Kane would soon arrive to discuss a very unusual development with them.

Mary was very excited. She couldn't stop smiling. She even giggled a bit. But she stopped when she saw Kane come through the door.

Kane looked somber.

Mary was confused again.

"Nothing could be harder," started Kane, "than telling all of you, who I consider my family, what I have to tell you. But first, please, be seated, make yourselves as comfortable as possible, and I'll have the bots bring something refreshing to drink." He motioned them toward the dayroom furniture on the other side of the room.

Mary, who, despite all the vomiting, had been feeling better than she'd felt in years, suddenly felt sick again, sick at heart.

Brooklyn sat next to her, awkwardly because of a bent leg brace, on a couch that cuddled them. "Eeee, I did desire that jiji and I might be better strangers." Suddenly he grabbed her hand. "Yet now I fear that, in pushing his way ahead of me for star prep, he doomed himself."

Mary squeezed Brooklyn's hand back and bit her lip. This wasn't turning out the way she'd expected at all.

The bots handed out something to drink.

Mary used hers to water a plant.

"Of course I'll have to call the colonel's daughter and let her know." Kane looked happy now.

Mary started to hope again.

"And his daughter will need a whole lot of support to get through this, which I will personally provide." Kane looked even happier.

Mary was confused again.

Kane looked down, his expression unreadable but his voice now somber. "Even though we're always totally diligent in our care of you, sometimes things that simply can't be foreseen or prevented go wrong. Most unfortunately I must tell you that our beloved colonel is dead."

"No!" Mary was on her feet.

Brooklyn pulled her back down, wrapping strong arms around her. Mary knew she now had the strength to fight those arms, but what was the point? She had made a literally fatal misjudgment when she saw that vial.

Maybe it was just as well that she was just a pathetic old woman in a nursing home, waiting for a death that should have come decades ago. Maybe it was just as well that she never was a star captain, that she never made it to the stars.

Colonel Jethro Hayes strained to stand up enough to see the results of the price sort for body parts. It was on the full-disclosure screen of the pink-panda bot on the other side of the lab. Jethro had just made a remarkable discovery: his legs were starting to work again.

If he could just stop puking...

Jethro squinted hard at the bot's screen. Kidneys! He should have known they'd take his kidneys first. He lowered himself back into his wheelchair and protectively pressed his back against it, then moved his lower legs. He might not need his wheelchair for long if he could just outwit this pink panda.

Weapon. He needed a weapon. He checked the trash can next to him.

Nothing but that empty vial, its label facing up. Apparently he was puking compliments of one Archibald A. Astor.

Surgical tray. Bunch of stuff that would do for flesh and blood, but not a bot.

Bot. What were their weaknesses?

Pink Panda was standing in front of an open insta-freeze, molding a receptacle so there would be enough room for two kidneys.

Greedy fuckin' bastard.

Jethro figured it wasn't worried about an old man in a wheelchair, puking his guts out behind it. Jethro could also see that it wasn't the strongest bot-model available, probably considered unnecessary in a nursing home. Still, no knees he could hit from behind. Same super-secure, flattened pear-shape all the bigger bots had. Very stable front and back.

What was as strong and substantial as this bot? What could come in low? He looked around the laboratory. Nothing.

The pink-panda bot's kidney receptacle was ready. It turned back toward Jethro, deploying a scalpel.

Still puking, Jethro gripped the sides of his wheelchair. Then it came to him.

The scalpel, reminding Jethro of an old pizza cutter, started to whir.

How to outwit a bot...

Jethro darted a look sideways toward the door, then made a break for it in his wheelchair. He knew he couldn't make it to the door before Pink Panda cut him off, but hoped the bot didn't know that he knew that.

The pink-panda bot turned its flatter side towards Jethro, its most unstable side as far as he could tell, to cut Jethro off before he reached the door.

While Jethro jerked the wheelchair in a new direction by stalling one wheel, he twisted himself out of it and sent it smashing into the side of the bot.

Its whirring scalpel hit the wheelchair, screaming as Pink Panda went down, half-shoved into the open insta-freeze.

Jethro ignored his shoulder, screaming with pain from hitting the floor, and rolled for the door.

The doorknob was too high for him to reach. He could hear the bot struggling to extricate itself from the insta-freeze behind him.

Come on legs... Atrophied muscles jerked, shook, and misfired.

Some kind of alarm went off.

Jethro got up on one very shaky knee, turned the knob, and fell into the hall. He looked at the door to the dayroom then looked away, searching for the closest window in the hall that led to it. A memory of Star Captain Mary, looking as if she understood what was going on, threatened his concentration, quickly followed by a memory of that boy Brooklyn cradling JFK. He wouldn't allow himself to think about them. Instead, he thought about—however stupidly—finding his lost Dukes-of-Hazzard car.

Jethro knew what he had to do, and it wasn't get back into the dayroom to be any kind of hero trying to help other patients anymore. He wasn't an old has-been in a wheelchair anymore. He needed to look out for number one.

Okay, that Brooklyn wasn't so bad but, damn, he was only a colored. And Star Captain Mary? Southern chivalry be damned; she was so nuts she probably wouldn't even know what was going on when they harvested her organs.

Jethro was outta there. He'd take his chances outside with Africa's wild lion clones.

Kane checked his palm, having to consciously unclench it to better read the latest page. Shimatta! What was wrong with that pink-panda lab bot that it kept just paging him instead of including a message with some actual information? Suddenly couldn't access the circuitry needed to type? Kane tried to imagine what news he was missing. Had that stupid bot voided the "puking" experiment again by adding another experiment as it had with JFK? Had it again failed to get the kidneys in time? Hidoi! Kane struggled to keep his irritation from showing in front of the patients over whom he just had to solidify his control. Now. Pink Panda would have to wait.

Kane kneeled next to the cuddle couch where Brooklyn was holding Star Captain Mary. "I know how hard this must be for you, Star Captain." He put a consciously relaxed hand on her knee. "You're suffering from survivor's guilt because you were originally going to get prepped next. But you have to understand that you're not responsible; you did nothing to contribute to the colonel's death."

Kane got to his feet and looked around the room at them all. "And what all of you have to understand is that Colonel Jethro Hayes didn't die in vain. What we've already learned from this tragedy will help billions in nursing homes everywhere."

But none of them were looking at him. They were looking behind him. Had he heard the staff-only door open? Had that stupid pink-panda lab bot finally come out because Kane hadn't answered its pages?

Funny, it didn't sound like a bot. It sounded like the faltering steps of a—

"Run!" It was the colonel's voice.

Kane spun around.

The colonel was on his feet, but just barely, clinging to the door frame. "None of us is going to the stars. They're just harvesting our organs."

Think! Kane screamed in his thoughts. He grabbed the dayroom bot and quickly typed some commands on his way toward the colonel. "Colonel! Let me help you!"

But now there were different faltering steps behind Kane. He about-faced into Brooklyn. Fortunately, their collision was too much for Brooklyn's bent leg brace, and he collapsed on the floor.

Sugoi, thought Kane, suppressing a smile. One down, one to—

But when he turned back toward the colonel that idiot Mary stood in his way with a huge grin. "Star Captain Mary, reporting for duty now that the new cadet's been prepped."

At least there shouldn't ever be any need to either risk, or waste the cost of, a forget-all injection on her.

"Maybe," Kane said, "you can help me with the cadet, Star Captain." Over her shoulder, behind the colonel, Kane thought he saw something moving in the staff-only hall.

Of course Mary was too stupid to get out of Kane's way so he could get to the colonel. And the colonel was struggling with shaky legs to turn around and check the staff-only hall behind him...where Kane was now sure he saw something moving.

Kane couldn't think of anything better to do, so he backhanded Mary out of his way. Strangely, given the force of the blow, she didn't go down. But it not only got Mary out of his way but got—as Kane had hoped—the colonel's attention away from the staff-only hall.

Kane heard something behind him in the dayroom again. That Brooklyn must have gotten back to his feet. Kane turned to look back over his own shoulder at the dayroom, just as he saw the colonel start to look over his shoulder at the staff-only hall again. But then Kane heard the sound he'd been waiting for.

He turned his attention away from the dayroom. The colonel was on the ground now, unconscious if not already dead. Though its motions indicated there was something dreadfully wrong with it, perhaps explaining the lack of messages accompanying those pages, Pink Panda had apparently managed to administer the injection Kane had ordered through the dayroom bot. Still behind the colonel, Pink Panda started to drag the colonel back into the staff-only hall, allowing the door to close behind them.

The only thing that was really bothering Kane now was the expression on Mary's face as she apparently tried, but failed, to get around him in time to make it through the closing door. But then she did the only thing she could have to banish any fear that she might actually understand what was happening.

She threw herself into Kane's arms. "What happened? I'm so confused. I don't understand! You've got to help me!"

Sugoi... Perfect opening for Kane, even if Mary was thrashing about so much in her distress that she was twisting him around backward until she would have been against the staff-only door herself.

But Brooklyn pushed himself between the door and Mary. "Last thing you want, fair maiden," Brooklyn said softly, "is to go in there. We can do nothing more, now, for the colonel."

Brooklyn, thought Kane, and the others, will have to be dealt with. It was Kane's job to do it without forget-all injections if he possibly could. Shimatta! Last thing he needed was for their relatives, who'd read all about the nursing-home scandals, to find holes in his patients' memories.

Kane took the opening Mary'd given him. "I know you're confused. And I have to apologize to all of you because what I told you before about the colonel already being dead was, well, a lie."

Marilyn gasped.

Napoleon frowned.

Brooklyn followed Kane as he led Mary back to the cuddle couch.

"As you now know, the colonel wasn't dead yet. But I was afraid that if I told you, you'd want to see him, and I wanted to spare you the final stages, the loss of his mind and the rampant paranoia you just witnessed."

"*Mauvaise honte*," Napoleon snorted, then nodded toward Mary. "That doesn't explain your striking a woman!"

"No, but I didn't know how else to get her away from the colonel quickly enough at the time. You see the other thing I didn't want to have to tell you about what went wrong with the star prep—which I will now explain in detail—is that it can be contagious. I love you all far too much to alarm you unnecessarily and, unfortunately, I didn't foresee the colonel making it back to the dayroom."

Now Marilyn snorted.

Napoleon quoted Napoleon, "Love does more harm than good."

SUE HOLLISTER BARR

Mary snuggled up to Kane as he and the cuddle couch caressed her, struggling mightily not to cringe at Kane's touch. He was going on, spinning his lies. She was hardly listening.

The colonel must be dead by now, since live organ harvesting wasn't worth the risk of a second escape. The bots might not be smart enough to figure that out, but Mary had failed to distract Kane when he started to type more commands into the rubber-ducky dayroom bot.

So sad. Especially because, unlike herself, the colonel had been perfectly lucid all along. Mary bit her lip, remembering him standing in the doorway covered with his own vomit but without his wheelchair. She'd seen the Archibald A. Astor vial in Kane's hand just before they took the colonel in to be "prepped for the stars." It was the exact same thing she'd gotten from that half-disassembled bot in the garbage dump that was Africa beyond their nursing home.

The vials had been marked for experimental use only. Mary had figured Kane was making extra money through human experimentation before he harvested organs and had no idea of the military powerhouse he'd unleash once he poured that vial down the colonel's throat. Clearly whatever miracles Archibald A. Astor had provided for Mary mentally he had provided for the colonel physically.

"...isn't that right, Star Captain Mary?"

Mary was glad she tuned back into Kane in time to look up with a smile and say, "Star Captain Mary, reporting for duty!"

"That's a good girl!" Kane patted Mary with a hand she wanted to bite.

Instead she kept her smile plastered on but looked at the others in the dayroom.

Napoleon. Completely in character with fingers tucked into the middle of his shirt. Mary wondered what his real name was. And what failures in his real life had led him, when his mind finally went, to latch onto the identity of Napoleon. Had he been a failure in the military?

Marilyn Monroe. Here Mary could guess. As old as this Marilyn Monroe was now, Mary could see she had always been thin with a sharply aristocratic face. The tall, elegant type, perhaps. Had she been passed over for some buxom bombshell?

And last in the dayroom with Kane at the time, the typical dayroom rubber-ducky bot.

"...isn't that right, Star Captain Mary?"

No, Rubber Ducky wasn't quite last. Mary looked down at the backs of her own hands, before answering Kane with a bright, chirpy, "Yes!" Her liver spots had all but disappeared. There were so few wrinkles left she may as well have been born in 2018 instead of 1948. Even for someone that much younger, her hands were beginning to look ridiculously young.

How long before someone noticed? Had anyone who'd seen the colonel out of his wheelchair and both the colonel and Mary puking started to suspect? For how long would the bots and Kane believe her Star-Captain-Mary act?

Star Captain Mary. The failures in her real life? Obvious. She'd never made it to the stars. It had been all she'd ever wanted, and she'd never made it.

"...but Jack is fine."

Bullshit!

But Marilyn seemed to be buying it. Hopefully she'd buy it when Kane also told her it was her turn to join Jack. Hopefully Napoleon would think he was going to command armies amidst the stars.

Boomers for the Stars. Mary realized she wasn't the only Boomer that line had worked on. She smiled wistfully as memories she hadn't been able to access for years flooded her. Boomers for the Stars... It had started in the early years of the century with Mars One's willingness to take settlers of any age, as long as they accepted that they could never return to Earth. It had picked up speed when the science of longevity was in its infancy, but post-World-War-II Baby

Boomers were the first generation to reap its benefits.

To grasp things mentally, to be able not only to remember but to piece things together. Mary felt like a person dying of thirst who'd just woken up in a reservoir. And where had this great mental thirst come from? Advances in longevity had been extensive enough to make its practitioners a fortune selling replacement organs that kept Boomers alive much longer that their wildest dreams. But not extensive enough to keep them in very good shape. A pig heart was great, but no one was going to pay for a pig brain.

And then there was the infamous Doomsday Decade, overflowing with irrefutable proof that nothing could be done to save humans except to evacuate Earth within the next fifty years. But nothing in Earth's solar system could accommodate such numbers, and who in their right mind would agree to the hardships of the interstellar travel needed to investigate alternatives?

The answer was people not in their right mind. People who were always confused, like Mary had been, whose vital signs could still be sent back to Earth to prove a distant planet was habitable. People now in their hundreds who—long after all those companies capitalizing on the infancy of longevity had pocketed the last of their life savings—had been sucking up the taxpayers' money to have their diapers changed.

Boomers for the Stars. It was very real at first. And even in the right mind Mary'd had at the time, she still wanted more than anything to go. But she'd failed even then.

Mary had tried so hard to do everything right. She'd followed her mama's mantra exactly, doing what she was told by others to do, always relying on others rather than exerting her own initiative. But she was told she'd flunked the personality test for lucid explorers.

And now all that was left of her dream was this shabby human-organ-harvesting facility—fronting as a nursing home—that still had the once-popular slogan of Boomers for the Stars for its name.

"Better now, Star Captain Mary?"

Mary smiled up at Kane and nodded.

"Be okay if I leave you with Rubber Ducky here?" he asked, nodding towards the dayroom bot. "It'll take good care of you." Insanely, Kane smiled, a smile that looked sexual. "I have to call the colonel's next of kin."

Mary nodded and smiled brightly, not having to fake it this time. He still thought she was the old, harmless, Star Captain Mary and was going to leave her in the dayroom with Rubber Ducky. This was the moment she'd been waiting for.

But she faked a last-minute change of heart—not pig but genuine enlarged-chimp in her case—suddenly frowning and clinging to Kane.

"There, there," he crooned. "Rubber Ducky will take very good care of you." Kane extricated himself and left.

Mary's chimp heart did yearn to push through the staff-only door behind him. But she told herself firmly that the colonel couldn't possibly still be alive and sat on her hands.

The cuddle couch responded by caressing her thighs.

Rubber Ducky offered another drink, which she again used to water a plant when Napoleon called the bot over to him.

In a heartbeat—chimp, pig, or human—Mary was out on the lawn.

SUE HOLLISTER BARR

Again, Jethro had to thank the combat reflexes that had made him a colonel. That half turn to look back over his shoulder, and his faking passing out when that insta-freezed panda missed with its injection, had saved him.

Still, getting out the window before that damn panda caught up with him had been a bitch. Especially since his fake passing out had included falling on his other shoulder, the one he hadn't fallen on in the lab, which had left him with two shoulders screaming with pain. And he'd had to stay on his other shoulder, feigning unconsciousness, till the bot dragged him close to a window. Getting across the lawn hadn't been easy either, though he had to smile over that part.

However difficult it was, he had crossed the lawn all the way to the fence on his feet. And through that fence he could see what passed for open land in Africa: one big garbage dump punctuated by the occasional, still-standing skyscraper. Amazing what happened when an entire continent's infrastructure collapsed.

Now if he could just find a weakness in a dirty silk fence so rickety it just had to have a weakness somewhere. He started testing it with one of his sore shoulders, cursing silently as he remembered a time when silk was only a fabric he could easily tear.

A memory intruded. Napoleon.

Jethro fought it off. An old soldier like Napoleon would understand that every battle had its casualties.

That shriveled old woman who thought she was Marilyn Monroe.

Jethro fought that off, too. Shame, but it couldn't be helped.

Brooklyn? Again, a colored...

A weakness in the fence! Jethro pushed through to the other side, even though it all but killed his shoulders.

On the other side of the Boomers-for-the-Stars fence, the garbage-strewn African landscape stretched out to the horizon in front of Jethro. He sniffed. Oddly, the refuse hardly smelled, picked clean by insects long ago. Salt... He imagined he could faintly smell the salt from the desalination plants still operating by the sea.

Like a good soldier, Jethro cast one last glance backwards through the nursing home's fence before starting down the road he knew led to the port.

Star Captain Mary. She was now out on the lawn as usual, probably about to settle down in front of the Boomers for the Stars sign and map her rocketship's trajectory between a red giant and a supernova. Jethro smiled softly at her through the fence, then choked back the part of him that wondered how many more times they'd let her out to live in her harmless fantasy world on the nursing home's lawn.

Resolute, he turned away and started down the road to the port.

Combat reflexes. He turned when he heard, ever so softly, what he knew was someone else testing the fence. But in a place Jethro had already tested that he knew had no weaknesses.

Dammit!

He'd almost said it aloud. Now Star Captain Mary was smashing her shoulder into a part of the fence Jethro knew she could never get through.

Jethro returned to the weakness in the fence he'd found and forced his way back through onto the nursing home's lawn. It hurt his shoulders twice as much going back in. But it was almost worth it to see the expression on Mary's face when she spotted him.

Mary ran into his arms, knocking him over because neither of them had taken into account how weak his legs were still. She was blubbering something about how bad she felt about leaving him and how sure she had been that he was dead.

He, with her on top of him, was realizing that his legs weren't the only part of him below the waist that felt young again.

She helped him to his feet, apologizing for knocking him down.

"Not at all," he said, not feigning sincerity. "This way, ma'am," he added with a flourish of his hand. But he stumbled badly as he headed back toward the weakness in the fence that would get both of them out this time.

"Allow me," she said quickly, wrapping his arm around her shoulder.

His shoulder screamed with pain at that, but it was almost worth it to feel her warmth against him again. "Thanks," he said. "Your mind. How—?"

"Archibald A. Astor. Same as your legs."

"When?"

"When I was missing. I got off the nursing home grounds. A defective bot must have stolen it off the cart bringing it here and sold me a vial."

Jethro had been keeping a wary eye on the nursing home, wishing like hell that he could move faster. "Remember when carts were called cars, and we still had trucks?"

"Yeah," she marveled. "Now I'm remembering a lot of things."

They'd reached the weakness in the fence. Jethro let Mary through first. There were still no signs of life from the nursing home, but that couldn't last. Jethro squeezed through, suddenly too proud to let Mary see how much it hurt his shoulders.

"Road toward the port?" she asked.

He nodded but frowned when she started down the same road he'd planned to take before, when he was alone. Somehow having her along changed things. He steered them onto the garbage by the side of the road, stretching as far as he could see with all the towering-but-crumbling buildings close by.

"You'll never be able to walk on this!" she objected.

"We're sitting ducks on the road," Jethro pointed out. "If you'll pardon the reference to our former dayroom staff."

Not very good but she smiled, which did all kinds of funny things to him. He actually felt giddy.

Then she picked something up out of the garbage they were plodding through and smiled at it. It took Jethro a long moment of confusion before he realized what he was feeling when he saw her smile at something other than himself. Insanely, he was feeling possessive and jealous. How stupid, he argued with himself. But his ridiculous feelings of possessiveness and jealousy just got stronger until they were so overwhelming he felt blinded to anything else.

"In Africa?" Mary marveled as they struggled over a broken table, looking at what she had picked up from the garbage. "This must really, literally, have fallen off a cart." She showed him a plastic replica of a Civil War soldier waving a Confederate flag.

Jethro found himself, to his utter amazement, hating even a Confederate soldier because she was looking at it and not him. With a mighty effort he finally managed to distract himself by thinking about her accent, now that she wasn't playing Star Captain Mary. "Virginia?"

She nodded, then squinted at him. "Georgia?"

He beamed, giddy again because she was looking at him. "Remember the Old South, the one still remembered and revered by our folks in the 1950s?"

He felt her stiffen at first, but then she smiled softly. "Outside, at night, was magic. The shrill song of the cicadas. The smell of freshly tilled earth. The stars. So bright and beautiful that it almost hurt to throw back your head and look at them. Silent. Serene. Infinite. All I ever wanted was to get to them." Her voice cracked.

He realized there was a price she was paying for remembering things. Time to get practical anyway. "Got any money?"

"No," she answered, somewhat testily as she struggled to get him over a discarded cart door.

Shit. Why hadn't his kids returned his phone calls? "Where were you going with no money?" He didn't think she had any family.

"Anywhere where being prepped for the stars doesn't mean losing all my saleable organs. Figured I'd live in the garbage like so many other people do. Also..." She trailed off.

"Also what?" Jethro asked.

"Well..."

"What?"

"The others..."

Jethro didn't have to ask what others she was talking about. "Out of it. Like you were. So they'll still believe it's star prep and won't fight the bots. They'll never know otherwise."

"Like JFK?"

Touché. Jethro didn't think she'd remember.

"And even if they never know otherwise, they still lose their lives."

"What lives? They don't even remember their own real names!"

"It's still a life! I know. I was there. Even if I thought I was Star Captain Mary out amidst the stars, it was still me, alive in that fantasy world...as if I was an actress forever on stage."

An intensity of feelings Jethro hadn't experienced since his youth washed over him. Bad feelings. This wasn't how it was supposed to go. She was supposed to be looking up to him for guidance. He was supposed to be supporting her physically, offering her his arm...rather than leaning on her with his arm over her shoulder because he could hardly walk. And they'd been walking for quite awhile like that. How did a woman ever get to be so strong? But then something occurred to him that gave him the edge over her after all. "And...how exactly were you going to help Napoleon and Marilyn by heading for the port?"

"You're not listening," she snapped, her face intense as she strained mightily to get him safely over a mountain of discarded chairs. "I have no money. Of what use could the port be to me? And I have no family, no friends. I gave up on the first group; the second group gave up on me. No future but to live in the garbage. At least at night I'll be able to see the stars. Besides..."

Jethro, in lot of pain, was feeling short-tempered, too. He rolled his eyes. "Besides?"

"That half-disassembled bot that sold me that vial of Archibald A. Astor's experimental drug. Maybe it has another two vials, one for Marilyn and one for—"

"That you'll be buying with what money?"

"That, somehow, I'll have to steal."

He heard the raw determination in her voice, felt her muscles tighten into steel. For a moment he forgot she was a woman and remembered all the brave men he'd had the honor of fighting with—and even, to give Charlie his due, against—in Nam.

And Jethro started thinking about Napoleon and Marilyn again, really thinking about them. "Dammit!" This time he knew he'd said it aloud.

Mary's voice softened. "Look, I get it. I realize it must be hard for you to understand, since you—" She cut herself off. "When were you born?"

"1946."

"Well over a hundred and you never lost your mind." She mimicked the hand flourish he'd given her earlier when he led her to the weakness in the fence. The perfect southern gentleman, except for the boob pressed against his rib cage. "I give you credit, sir, and a whole lot of it. Yours must be a strong mind, indeed."

That felt good...along with the boob.

"So it must be difficult for you to grasp what it's like for all of us who did lose our minds when we were the first generation to live so much longer than our ancestors had. Your not choosing to risk your life to go back to save Marilyn and Napoleon is easily forgivable..."

Jethro was feeling safe now, understood. But just then...

Combat reflexes. He felt something in her muscles, like she was about to pounce. Jethro was a good soldier, and a good soldier never relaxes completely.

Mary, and her boob, pulled away from him. She took his arm off her shoulder, leaving him to stumble a bit, making a fool of himself until he steadied himself by grabbing the leg of yet another upside-down table. She turned to face him and gave him a hard stare. "But Brooklyn has always been every bit as lucid as you are."

She was comparing him to the colored boy? And she was from the Old South, too, so why was she even concerning herself with—

"He's young."

So that was why. Jethro was remembering stories his grandfather used to tell him of plantation wives who tried to keep up with the men's visits to the slave quarters and gave birth to colored babies. The fathers, those bucks, were young. Unlike old, crippled Jethro. A riot of jealous and possessive feelings crashed over him.

Then he remembered Brooklyn flirting with his young daughter. Blind fury took full possession of him.

"You saw how he tried to save JFK," Mary said.

"Dammit! Dammit!" Jethro remembered Brooklyn with JFK; how could he forget? Mary was right. The only reason Brooklyn wasn't escaping the nursing home with them now was because, of the three of them, Brooklyn was the only one the bots had given the fuhgeddaboudit injection to after the JFK incident. Jethro realized he was wrong, realized he was letting his adolescent feelings of jealousy and possessiveness about Mary distort his thinking.

But then Jethro saw the tear on Mary's cheek...for Brooklyn! And another swarm of new feelings he couldn't fully understand or control took over. For a moment he knew they didn't make much sense, then he was convinced he'd been played. Mary had never loved him. A little voice in him still asked what love had to do with it, but some demon in him silenced it.

Brooklyn. All she wanted from Jethro was that he risk, and probably lose, his life saving her colored lover.

"He's young," Mary said again. "He has his whole life ahead of him."

"He's nothing but a worthless nigger."

Mary leaped back as if Jethro had leprosy. "Georgia. I should have known." She looked stricken, as if he'd lynched someone—a thing he'd never do—then, crying, turned and left him.

Jethro didn't move. He let her go.

SUE HOLLISTER BARR

Kane smirked, thinking about Star Captain Mary. Still safely out of her mind. Probably just wandered off again like that time they found her covered with vomit.

Vomit... Something about vomit... Kane felt he should be remembering something but was distracted when he felt the tickle in his palm of an incoming message.

The colonel was quite another matter, he thought, ignoring the message. Shimatta! That hidoi jiji could cause real trouble. Why hadn't his daughter returned Kane's calls?

Kane had also been calling in every favor he could think of, incognito messaging everyone he knew. Why had he let the colonel

live so long anyway? So he could savor
saving the opportunity to hit on his daughter
by announcing his death and then supporting
her through the trauma? When it turned out
she wouldn't even return his calls?

Kane flipped his palm and stretched it
to read the new message. Then smiled. Didn't
have to worry about the colonel getting to his
next of kin with a full report about Kane's
nursing home any more. Shame about the
daughter, who was really hot, but the son's cart
had been found in the garbage on the way to
the port just after they left Boomers for the
Stars. Everyone in organ harvesting knew the
roads weren't safe, especially for younger
people, ne? It happened all the time. The son
and daughter hadn't yet been found, but, when
they were, they'd probably have fewer organs
left than JFK.

Speaking of which... Kane leaned over
to examine the pink panda still twitching at his
feet. Illegal disposal should work fine,

because the first part of Kane's cover story about how his lab bot got damaged before just wandering off was well-documented. But even with the illegal disposal that should render its records unrecoverable, Kane would have to wipe its memory clean before he shut it down for good. Just in case it was ever found in the garbage.

First, Kane wanted to recover some information for himself.

And then there was the staff-only security door and Brooklyn. In fairness to the door, Brooklyn's records showed he had a tech background that included a whole lot of hacking. Still, it hadn't been comforting to find him on the other side of that door, too. So hidoi...

But ultimately, beyond all these petty annoyances, there was the question of Archibald A. Astor. Kane was no fool. He'd seen enough when he tested Archibald A. Astor's vials on first JFK and then the colonel.

Vomiting aside, and unless there was some later-developing side effect, Archibald A. Astor's vials actually worked!

Kane thought he remembered those vials coming from the U.S.A., ground zero for research into such things. But from some hobbyist who couldn't afford to field test anywhere better than Boomers for the Stars? Had he stolen it? What kind of name was Archibald A. Astor anyway? Probably made it up to protect the guilty.

Kane's human heart wouldn't last forever and he, in the thick of unregulated organ harvesting, knew better than to get either a synthetic, animal, or even ultra-expensive human transplant if it could be avoided. And what about his mind?

Another message tickled his palm. Rubber Ducky in the dayroom. Kane gave the admin security door a disdainful look on his way out.

Was it his imagination or did Marilyn Monroe give him a sharp look? But then Kane saw what Rubber Ducky had messaged about. Marilyn looked green and proceeded to spit up into a nearby planter.

Napoleon didn't just have his fingers tucked into the middle of his shirt; he was holding his gut with both hands.

Brooklyn, hand over his own mouth, gave Kane a sheepish look.

An outbreak of stomach flu?

Just what Kane needed. But he managed to look affectionate, surprised to find "Miss Monroe" was so sick she cringed away from him when Kane tried to stroke her.

"My fault," said Brooklyn, before spitting up.

Stomach flu that Brooklyn had first?

Kane got his act together. "I just came out to reassure you that Rubber Ducky will do all necessary to keep you comfortable. Don't worry; these things are generally short-lived."

With that he wheeled back through that inadequate security door and escaped to his office.

His messages were being answered. Pieces were coming together. He stared at his safe long enough for it to recognize his retinas and open.

But nothing happened.

Shimatta! Always something!

Mary had been six. Her only friend was what Mary's family, some of whom had been born in the 19th century, called a "pickaninny." Mary wasn't sure what her friend's real name was, because her friend answered to whatever anyone called her, and people called her all kinds of things.

Mary didn't think it was polite to keep asking her friend about her name, especially since her friend looked very uncomfortable every time Mary did. So

Mary called her Rithmatic, because her friend was very good at math.

Rithmatic also looked very uncomfortable when there were other people around, so they'd play out back in a gully behind the farmhouse. No one could see them, but they were close enough to hear and answer back if anyone called.

Mary told Rithmatic about how she was going to the stars. Rithmatic told Mary that the reason the stars were so pretty was because they had great, beautiful cities circling them. Together they built elaborate models of what these cities looked like out of whatever they could get their hands on. Their masterpiece was a city they named

Sparkle because of the glitter Rithmatic found to cover all its rooftops.

But sometimes they couldn't avoid other people. Mary's family would smile down at Rithmatic and start telling jokes: "What does the old colored man say if you ask him, 'What's eight plus eight?'"

Rithmatic would look down at the ground, silent.

Someone in Mary's family would answer, "Why he says, 'Don't rightly know, sah, but ate plus ate must be mighty full.'"

Everyone in Mary's family would laugh. Everyone in Rithmatic's family would smile and nod their heads, especially Rithmatic's father.

Rithmatic's father was the old colored man Mary's family told jokes about. He looked old enough to be Rithmatic's grandfather. He was all bent over and covered with really nasty looking scars. But he owned a gas station much bigger than the one Mary's uncle owned.

One summer night Mary's uncle threw a huge party in a clearing in the woods. The sounds of laughter snaked through the woods, along with the smell of fresh corn fritters. Dancing could be seen between the trees. Bonfires blazed, blocking out the stars.

Mary and Rithmatic weren't supposed to go, but for some reason Rithmatic insisted on going. Even though she didn't look too happy about it.

When they reached the last tree before the clearing, they saw Rithmatic's father swinging round and round by his neck. Kicking furiously, he spotted Mary and Rithmatic. Though barely conscious with his hands tied behind his back, he gestured wildly for them to go back into the woods.

Mary's family was calling Rithmatic's father the same name the colonel called Brooklyn.

Something in the African garbage Mary was walking through now caught her foot, then wiggled. She looked down to see her toes caught in a tiny purple-pug bot's skin folds. It's full-disclosure screen half flickered to life, flashing something about the penalties for illegally disposing of any bot. Then it identified its owner as some guy named Andy, on a layover between launches at the port, before flickering off. After that the eyes, which were even more cheaply made than the threadbare purple fur, struggled through several abortive attempts before closing. The bot was still.

Mary extricated her toes and moved on, but not without realizing what had been niggling at the edge of her consciousness ever since the colonel had led her back into all this trash. No signs of life. Where were all the people who lived in the garbage?

She stopped, leaning against the upturned chassis of a faux-1956 Thunderbird, from the days when hydrogen cars sought acceptance by mimicking old American dream cars. The sun slanted low between two crumbling buildings, lending their now-fuzzy silk exteriors a peachy glow.

Mary squinted toward the sun, thinking she saw someone run between the ends of the buildings. She leaned away from the T-bird and waded through the trash to catch up. All but blinded by the sun's glare, the closer she got, the surer she was that she was hearing some kind of commotion. She finally turned the corner, no longer looking west, so she was again able to see.

A swarm of people ebbed and flowed against the end of one building like insects crawling all over each other, their numbers so great that the lack of people in the garbage was no longer a mystery. Everyone seemed to be struggling to get to one spot with a mounting sense of urgency that built up to a desperate frenzy. People started calling out the time at one minute before the hour and then looking up.

Windows opened high in the fuzzy-silk building, now a brilliant apricot as the sun began to set. Garbage rained down. People below cried out in pain when hit and with pleasure and victory in their voices when they caught something. Fights broke out. A woman rushed toward Mary, carrying half a loaf of bread. She switched it to the arm farther away from Mary, glaring as she passed and ran on. Mary looked up at the people in the building, still throwing garbage out the windows.

Her mama's mantra echoed in her mind, "You can't do anything in this world unless you mind what others say. You can't do anything a'tall without the help of others."

Mary had rejected everything else she got from growing up in the Old South as soon as she was old enough. But this one mantra from her mother had been repeated so often it felt like it had been carved into her bones. Mary had always followed it religiously. What she figured she had to do now was to get the help of those people in the building. They could tell her what to do. They could tell her how to report the situation at Boomers for the Stars to the proper authorities. Mary had only stressed Brooklyn to the colonel because she thought the colonel would have more sympathy for a fellow lucid patient. But, with the help of the people in this building, Mary should be able to save all the patients still in Boomers for the Stars.

Unfortunately, the people in the building were too high up to hear if she called to them, and Mary's retinas wouldn't open any doors that still worked.

She circled the decrepit building, hoping for a door that either didn't work or was already open. Laughing children danced around her, as adept at darting about in the garbage as mountain goats. They were tantalizing and teasing each other with whatever food they'd caught from the windows. Sunset washed over their happy faces, making even the trash around them look golden.

Mary spotted the top of a door that appeared to be ajar, though she couldn't be sure in the failing light, and it was barely visible behind the rubble. Getting to it was all but impossible. Even the children gave up and abandoned her, their calls and laughter fading into the background as one pretended to be a lion clone chasing the others.

When Mary got to the door, she felt around in the darkness beneath the debris and found the door was ajar—but not enough for her to get in. She had to dive into the garbage, wedging bigger pieces of trash in the opening until she could finally squeeze herself through.

"Can't say I was expecting company."

It took Mary's eyes a moment to adjust to even less illumination. Flickering light just barely revealed the face of her host. He was staring at her from across a wide space that glinted here and there of huge, solid, vertical screens lining its aisles. Mary steadied herself with a hand on what she realized was the checkout counter of a now-defunct supermarket.

"And we're all out of Cocoa Puffs."

Mary smiled. "My favorite for a long, long time. How did you know?" She made her way down an aisle, tripping over rubble in the dark. But as she got closer she could see her host better. A man about her age.

He was squinting at her. "In your forties?"

Was it the light, or Archibald A. Astor? "I was born in 1948."

At that he jumped. "Just arrived here after a new treatment you got in the States?"

"Beat the rush to immigrate to Africa by coming early for the space program. Never left."

His puzzled look was illuminated by the flickering light Mary could now identify as a tiny newsfeed in the bottom corner of an old supermarket screen. She looked closer when she thought she caught something about Archibald A. Astor, but it turned out to be a prominent, red-headed scientist named Andrew Adams, who was missing. Then she noticed a snarl of something she hadn't seen in a long time poking out from the underside of the huge vertical screen.

"Is that an...alligator clip?"

"What they used to call 'hard-wired.' So out-of-date now they've all but stopped protecting against it." He caressed a tangle of cables. "This baby could hack into anything from a bot to a C-2 launcher."

With the light from the screen flickering over him at close range, Mary looked him over. He was dressed in a torn, faded "one suit for life" prototype that couldn't decide what color had been requested. It was flickering through all possible colors, oddly in sync with the

colors on the newsfeed screen. Thick
material had been tied around his feet
instead of shoes. Mary decided he
probably wouldn't be able to help her
reach the proper authorities to help the
patients still in Boomers for the Stars.
"So how do I get to the people upstairs?"

"The ones with the suppliable
supermarket? You must really be
desperate for those Cocoa Puffs..."

Marilyn, Napoleon, Brooklyn...
Mary was desperate. "How?"

He shrugged, then nodded toward
the back of the store. "There's an
elevator that still works in there
somewhere..."

Mary walked around him and headed into the dark, thankful for the light from his newsfeed for as long as it lasted.

Something squealed and ran over one of her feet. Mary thought it best to ignore it.

She was running out of light now but—was it wishful thinking? She stood still and waited for the newsfeed behind her to flash an image with lots of white. Yes, the glint off elevator controls up ahead.

Dark. So dark now. Mary touched the wall next to her. Silk, like the building's exterior. She trailed her fingers over its bumps, pocks, and tears as she headed toward where she thought she'd seen the elevators.

Light. Up ahead. And some noise, rhythmic and slow. As she approached she thought she saw a teeny room, with some bedding strewn over the floor. Up close she realized it was the inside of an elevator. The noise was the door, which kept trying—unsuccessfully—to close. The light came from a standard-issue solar lantern, which illuminated another snarl of wires with alligator clips. Mary couldn't help but wonder how Mr. Cocoa Puffs managed to get any sleep with that damn door trying to close all night.

Mary backed out. By the light of the solar lantern she could just barely make out that she was in a foyer with a maze of elevator-lined hallways leading out of it in all directions. As she moved farther away from the solar lantern, she again trailed her fingers over the foyer's walls to guide herself to each hallway of elevators.

Dark. All dark. To be sure she pressed any controls she could feel, but nothing happened, and some even crumbled at her touch.

Marilyn, Napoleon, Brooklyn... Who was going to save them? She remembered that pink-panda bot cutting off JFK's hand. Then she remembered Rithmatic's father swinging from that tree and had to blink back tears.

Was light illuminating something just around the next corner, or was it only a mirage created by her desperation? Mary hurried, sure she could have, thanks to Archibald A. Astor, broken into a run if she could have seen enough to make it safe.

She turned the corner.

A thin slice of light from underneath an elevator door illuminated what must once have been a magnificent faux-marble floor. Gingerly, Mary felt for the controls and pressed. The door opened, letting out a blaze of light that blinded her.

Mary stepped in anyway, one foot in and one foot out till her eyes adjusted. 250 floors, though this elevator only serviced some. How high had those people throwing garbage out the windows been? Then she got an idea and stood to the side of the controls till the light showed the very few floor buttons that weren't dusty, and picked one, thankful that they had actual, physical buttons.

Jethro spat and shook like a wet dog, trying to rid himself of the salt as he pushed through the door. But clouds of it swirled over the heads of everyone else who'd tracked it into the airpad. Still, it was better than the salt snowing down from all the desalination plants outside. Jethro didn't think he'd ever wax poetic about the briny sea again.

Flakes of salt still tickled the inside of his nose as he passed row upon row of those cheap little purple-pug bots they always sold at airpads. Hell, half of them looked broken already, and all of their purple fur was already threadbare.

Bots... Rubber Ducky... It hit him yet again, like a punch in the gut. Mary... He had been so, so wrong.

It had been all those damn feelings he hadn't felt in so long, like experiencing adolescence all over again. Unbelievably intense sexual attraction corrupting and exaggerating everything. Enough to make a young—or apparently an old—man crazy.

He found an orange bot, though the "Tickets Here" floating above it was barely visible through the clouds of salt.

"How much to the moon?" Jethro asked, fingering the money in his pocket. The old song started up in his head, "Fly me to the moon, and let me play among the stars."

"How many travelling?" verbalized the bot.

Jethro bit his lip.

"How many travelling?" repeated the bot.

Jethro bit his lip again. "Five."

The bot's full-disclosure screen flashed the cost for several different classes of service.

Jethro figured they'd have to have a class that didn't include air to breathe for him to be able to take not only himself and Mary but Marilyn, Napoleon and Brooklyn.

"Any subsidized tickets if you sign on for helium-3 mining?"

The bot's screen refreshed. Better, he could cover himself and Mary, but not the other three.

"Dammit!"

And where the fuck were his kids?

"Will you be purchasing any tickets at this time?" the bot asked.

"When are the next launches?"

The screen refreshed.

"I'd like to reserve five subsidized seats with a deposit, balance payable before departure."

"I'm sorry," started the bot.

Jethro didn't bother listening to the rest. He already knew they only accepted full payment for reservations to the moon but had figured it was worth a try. He walked away.

Where was he going to get the rest of the money?

How was he going to get the other three out of Boomers for the Stars?

Would he be able to find Mary?

"Hey, buddy, can you spare a kidney?"

Very funny. Jethro started to push past the bum. Then again...

One kidney on the black market...

"How much?"

The bum had moved on, apparently not expecting a response, then looked startled but quickly recovered. "Buddy, I'd sure like to pay you a whole lot more, but you see it's for my dying—"

"Daughter, I know. How much?"

The price given would have them all playing among the stars.

"Surgery here? In the open with witnesses? So you can't get greedy and take the other kidney and my heart, too?"

The bum backed, emptied his pockets into a shredder with shaking hands, and ran for the door.

The shaking hands must have affected his aim. A stack of intact unicards had landed on the floor. Jethro toed them apart idly, sick at heart as he saw each smiling ID pic of those destined to share the same fate as JFK. His heart stopped when he saw the last one. It was his daughter.

Jethro discovered that, thanks to Archibald A. Astor, he could not only walk but run. "Wait! Wait!"

The bum took off like a launcher.

Jethro discovered that he could not only run, but run fast. "I really need the money! It's okay if you don't do the surgery in the open!"

The bum slowed then turned, squinting at Jethro.

"You...you have just one location where you do the surgery?" Jethro asked. "On...all your clients?"

The bum shrugged convincingly before answering, "Yeah, why?"

"Just wanted to be sure it wasn't one of those any-convenient-back-alley deals," Jethro lied. "So unsanitary." His daughter. Had his son's unicard made it into the shredder? At least Jethro would be brought to the same location. If only it wasn't too late.

Kane loved the rich people still living in that tall building. Shame there were so very few of them left to sell organs to. His palm positively tingled from all their new-message tickles. Yabai! He'd been so busy reading their answers to all his incognito messaging that he hadn't even had time to worry about the safe he could no longer open.

With the African infrastructure all but gone, these few remaining "people in high places" had all the power—and the best intel. Calling in favors from the rich was so sugoi!

True, the colonel was still loose and could talk. But the reasonable certainty that the colonel's kids had been organ-harvested quieted Kane's fears that anyone would take such talk all that seriously.

Still, Kane wasn't getting enough on Archibald A. Astor. Before he got that safe open and drank one of those miracle vials himself—and started puking his guts out—he wanted to know a whole lot more.

Frustrated by a still-incoming message from one of his clients in "high places," Kane bent just the top of his thumb to toggle from text to voice. "The absolute earliest record you can find of this full-grown person only dates back a few weeks, ne?"

There was the usual delay, waiting for the other person to toggle to voice, then, "Konnichiwa! And even that's not reliable, coming as it does from koitsu, one of those ridiculous purple-pug bots at the airpad."

"Still have the purple-pug bot?" Kane asked.

"Never did. Intel from airpad feeds."

"GPS puts that bot where now?" Kane asked.

"Nowhere. Decommissioned."

Kane kicked the almost decommissioned pink-panda bot still at his feet. "Properly recycled?"

"Eeeee..." This was followed by laughter.

Kane kicked Pink Panda harder. "Kuso! Illegal disposal." He didn't think it would help loosen his client's tongue, but played his last card. "So...how's that sugoi human heart I gave you working?"

"My donor was under thirty, right?"

"Right," Kane lied. Amazing how long that Boomer had made it with his own heart.

"Just re-checking, since you never gave me the donor's name so I could check myself, ne? You know how much I love extreme sports."

"I know. And you know how much I love supplying you with anything that can help you," Kane cooed.

"Nanpa!" was the only half-kidding accusation of insincerity. "But still, even with all these super hi-power screens at my disposal, all my vast array of intel, what little I've got on Archibald A. Astor all goes back to that purple pug. Not reliable."

Kane's palm double-tickled. His rubber-ducky bot was messaging from the dayroom again. "Gotta go," Kane said, toggling back from voice to text. But he ignored Rubber Ducky.

Instead Kane started typing into Pink Panda again: "Archibald A. Astor vials, undesirable side effects."

Kane had to jiggle the panda to get it to respond. Shame he'd had to inflict more damage in addition to what the insta-freeze had done. But otherwise Pink Panda would be able to call for help when Kane wiped its memory clean.

The first jiggle did nothing, so Kane jiggled again.

"Initial vomiting necessary to expedite mass expulsion of defective tissue being replaced and..."

Jiggle.

"...preliminary projections predict one subsequent..."

Jiggle.

"...comatose period while certain restorative processes are finalized. Time between initial ingestion and comatose period varies widely depending on subject."

Hmmm. Didn't sound too bad. Kane typed: "Archibald A. Astor, vendor country of origin."

"Africa."

Funny. He could have sworn those vials had come from the U.S.A.

Rubber Ducky was messaging him again. He ignored it again and typed into Pink Panda: "Archibald A. Astor, product purpose."

Jiggle.

"Fountain of Youth."

Not exactly standard scientific jargon, but what could he expect from a Boomers-for-the-Stars client.

Rubber Ducky again.

Kane tried "Archibald A. Astor, vendor current location."

Jiggle.

Jiggle.

Jiggle.

"Shimatta!" Kane kicked the panda aside and, just for the hell of it, tried staring at the safe again, preparing to kick it, too.

It opened.

Funny, he thought he'd remembered right where he'd left the Archibald A. Astor package, but no. He finally found it on a completely different shelf. Kane swiped aside the lab request to get to all the vials he knew were left.

There weren't any at all left.

"Shimatta! Shimatta! Shimatta!"

Rubber Ducky again.

Kane headed for the lab. Checked everywhere. No Archibald A. Astor vials except the empty one they'd given the colonel.

Kane went back into his office, squatted next to Pink Panda and typed, "Archibald A. Astor, location Boomers for the Stars vials." Jiggled. Nothing.

Kane checked his messages. Nothing new, except all the unread messages from Rubber Ducky, who, fortunately, seemed to have at last given up.

He thought he heard something faint but strange somewhere outside his office. He ignored that, too.

Finally he made his way to the security door and went through it into the dayroom, more out of a bored restlessness than anything else.

Rubber Ducky was upside down in the cuddle couch, which was caressing it feverishly.

Kane looked everywhere, in every room. All of the patients were gone.

Mary's stomach lurched with the first upward rush of the elevator.

At least she wasn't vomiting any more.

At least she should be on her way to the people who'd thrown food down for the garbage dwellers and must be able to help Mary help the other patients still in the nursing home.

As the elevator continued to accelerate, it shuddered so violently Mary feared it would break apart. But then it settled into a stable zoom upwards. Her ears popped.

At least Mr. Cocoa Puffs had been right about there being an elevator in this great, tall derelict of an African building that still worked.

Cocoa Puffs... Mary smiled, now able to remember the few sweet memories she had of the American South. From an early age her every breakfast, every mid-morning snack, every little something to take the edge off her hunger while waiting for dinner to be ready, was always the same. Her mama would give her Cocoa Puffs.

The elevator started to slow, shuddering a bit more as it did so.

Her mama... Mary remembered her Virginian accent and that lyrical voice always telling Mary what to do.

The elevator stopped with a sickening lurch. Its doors opened to reveal a young woman in a dull green asymmetrical suit with a black hat covering her hair. Apparently she'd been waiting for the elevator, but at the sight of Mary she jumped back in disgust, exclaiming, "Dasai! Just where did you escape from?" Her voice was commanding. Still, was it Mary's need or imagination or did that voice also have the same lyricism as Mary's mama's?

Mary stepped out onto the floor where the woman had been waiting. Gone was any hint of decay; all was immaculate and new. "From a nursing home," Mary answered her. "Where the patients are used for medical experimentation, and then their organs are harvested. I need to report it to the proper authorities so they can save the patients who are still there." Mary remembered her mother's mantra. "But I can't do it without your help. Please help me!"

The woman already had a delicately shod foot in the elevator and seemed a bit taken aback, mumbling something Mary couldn't hear except that it started with "wagamama." But then the woman rallied and said "of course" in that lyrical voice.

Mary smiled.

The woman stepped back out of the elevator and ushered Mary down the hall. Here, like in the nursing home, the wallpaper featured faces with eyes that were supposed to follow a person walking by. But here the eyes worked. And the tasteful, subdued portraits looked like people of substance—people in control. Appearing to watch over her, they gave Mary confidence in the success of her mission.

They passed a supermarket, functional—unlike the one on the ground floor where she'd found Mr. Cocoa Puffs hacking into a newsfeed. A few shoppers, also in dull-colored asymmetrical suits, ran their hands over its vertical screens, making their selections. Mary detected a grace and dignity in the flow of both their clothes and their motions, reminding her of the aristocratic bearing of the "landed gentry" in Virginia long ago. Yet, like those ancient landed gentry she remembered from childhood, these younger counterparts seemed a bit absurd, somehow, since there were so few of them left in such a huge supermarket and such a vast Africa.

The woman with Mary hurried her along, nodding toward some impressive-looking offices at the end of the hall. "They'll help you," she said, apparently anxious to get Mary off her hands. "Though why someone your age is in a nursing home is beyond me, ne?"

"I was born in 1948."

"Nanpa!" The woman accompanied her laugh with a dismissive hand gesture.

"Really," Mary said. "Have you ever heard of a researcher named Archibald A. Astor?"

The woman froze. "What's the name of your nursing home?"

"Boomers for the Stars."

A kindly looking man in a uniform came out of the offices at the end of the corridor, started toward the supermarket, then spotted them and gestured back toward the offices. "Watashi no jimusho. Were you headed there?"

"Kesshite!" the woman said. "No, not at all."

Mary didn't understand the Japanese but watched as the man turned away from the offices again, bowed to them, moved on, and disappeared into the supermarket.

The woman then looked around quickly before pulling Mary away from the offices, too. They turned, going back down the hall the same way they'd come, and headed for an all-but-hidden door that dilated open with a hiss.

Beyond the door a spiral staircase loomed. Mary suspected extensive custom renovations. They clattered up the stairs to be met by another dilating door that let them out on another floor.

"The elevator doesn't stop here," the woman explained.

This floor had a lot that was impressive, including massive halls that shimmered with subdued light, but it had no offices, impressive or otherwise.

The woman led Mary through a huge wooden door.

Beyond it stretched a room that sported the largest collection of screens Mary had ever seen. They hovered in the air like clouds continually riddled by lightning. Those Mary could see alternated between extreme sports and tracking people.

Some of the people being followed appeared to be walking through snow. The others were in a building Mary finally recognized as the airpad at the port where she'd first set foot in Africa so very long ago. Next to each person an inset scrolled through bot data. Above the inset was an icon for the cheap purple-pug bots they apparently still sold everyone arriving at the airpads.

The screen nearest Mary advertised the opportunity to fight a cloned gorilla bare-handed. The screen next to it featured different locations for climbing sheer cliff faces. The one after that showed a frozen shot of someone at the airpad shielding his face from the camera. His purple-pug-bot inset flashed some kind of error message. But what caught Mary's eye was the name the screen gave for him: Archibald A. Astor.

Voices... The woman with Mary had joined a man at the far end of the room where colossal windows allowed the still-

setting sun to spill across the wooden
floor.

"Hidoi," spat the man. "Not reliable.
The rest of you are not reliable. Why else
would you bring some escapee from who-
knows-where in here, ne?"

"She's from Boomers for the
Stars!" the woman shouted, her voice
losing some of its lyricism.

But Mary tuned them out.
Gingerly she reached out to the screen
featuring Archibald A. Astor.

No one stopped her.

What if she couldn't find that
defective bot in the trash that sold her the
Archibald A. Astor vial again? Maybe
here was where she could find a way to get
more vials so those poor souls left in the

nursing home wouldn't spend the rest of their days thinking they were Marilyn Monroe and Napoleon Bonaparte.

Mary tapped the "about" icon on the Archibald A. Astor screen, hoping for contact information. Error message. She tried a few other icons with the same results. Finally she tapped what looked like an unlabeled custom icon.

She thought she might be denied access, or at least noticed by the man and the woman on the other side of the room. But they stood facing each other by the windows, set on fire by the sunset as their whispered argument hissed and crackled.

Just as Mary decided tapping the unlabeled custom icon wasn't going to do anything either, multiple sub-screens entitled "AAA" appeared in front of her.

The first sub-screen covered a boy-genius childhood so sheltered it didn't even include exposure to the Japanese craze everyone else's childhood did, at least in most generations that followed Mary's. A real babe in the woods, she thought as she started to brush that screen aside. But grotesque pictures of his ancient parents stopped her. Reclusive pioneers in longevity, their gentle natures wouldn't allow them to conduct tests on others. Multiple tests on themselves created a cacophony of agonized deformities before death finally spared them further pain. Their young son "AAA" swore he'd find the fountain of youth that had been so horribly elusive for his parents.

The next screens covered a roller coaster of AAA's brilliant scientific successes followed by crushing defeats in attaining the recognition his successes deserved. These last Mary attributed to AAA's extraordinary naiveté. But she brushed all of this aside, too, till she got to his final product, his fountain of youth.

Figuring she already knew about the vomiting, Mary brushed aside a screen about the side effects. As she did so something about coma caught her eye, but it was too late to recover that screen, and she thought that had been for an earlier version of the formula anyway. The next screen covered long-term goals and results, complicated stuff about essentially, eventually replacing every cell with its ideal version. Mary's fingers shoved it aside. All she had to do was to think of all the things she could now remember, including the sight of that despicable racist from the nursing home out of his wheelchair, to know what the stuff in that vial could do. The only thing that concerned her, other than how to get more vials, was how permanent the effect would be. When she got to that part she slowed down.

A hand fell on her shoulder. "If it works at all, the effect should be permanent."

Mary turned to look behind her.

The woman with the lyrical voice and the man by the windows were still talking among themselves at the other end of the room, voices low.

The man who had spoken to Mary stood behind her, a slow but infectious grin spreading over his freckled face as he peered into hers. "Are you really from Boomers for the Stars?" Even his hair looked on fire—what they used to call "carrot top"—as he looked at Mary in wonder. Obviously forgetting himself, he began to run his fingers over any parts of Mary not covered by clothing.

"Andy?" the man by the windows called across the huge room, his voice tinged with disbelief.

The man next to Mary looked up.

"Andy!" cried the woman. "Eeee... You're the last person I'd expect to see here at this time of day; you're always on the roof watching the sunset!"

Mary remembered the red hair from Mr. Cocoa Puffs' newsfeed. "Andrew Adams?" she asked. "The missing scientist?"

He looked boyishly sheepish, then held out his hand to Mary. "Andy to my friends."

Mary shook his hand but then frowned. "But what's your connection to Archibald A. Astor?"

"My middle name's Austin. At least I kept the AAA motif."

"Why not just keep your real name?"

He didn't look so boyish anymore. Instead he looked like a veteran of some particularly dreadful war. "Big Pharma."

"Back in the States?"

He nodded sadly but then brightened when the other two joined them from the windows, one on either side of him. Andy put an arm around each of them. "But here in Africa I'm getting this breakthrough tested, and these good folk will help me get it released! No more threats to my life. I'll no longer have to run and hide." He paused to give the man and the woman an affectionate squeeze. "I'm so lucky they found me when I was hiding!"

But it had all finally sunk in and Mary couldn't see through her tears...of gratitude. It was enough to account for how unbelievably faint she felt, but she fought it off and threw her arms around this man who had given her so much.

"There's a lot I don't understand, like why the proper authorities in the States wouldn't be the right place for you to have gone for help. But I can never, ever thank you enough, for giving me back my life, my memories, all I have ever been."

Completely overcome, Mary took his face between her hands and started kissing his freckles, one by one.

Suddenly everything, even the screens and the sunset, vanished. In the dark Mary couldn't tell if she was standing, sitting, or lying down. Or even whether her eyes were open or shut.

SUE HOLLISTER BARR

Jethro kept asking questions about how sanitary the removal of his kidney was going to be while the bum led him through the garbage-strewn landscape. Jethro went on and on about how he had to eyeball the equipment that would be used before any money changed hands. But the Vietnam veteran was really thinking about muscle memory. How well would the body of a man who had been in a wheelchair for so long remember the martial-arts training he'd gotten in the Marines? How many combatants, human and/or bot, would there be at their destination?

And, with the bum already throwing out IDs at the airpad, would it be too late to save his kids?

Though he didn't let on, Jethro knew the bum was taking him around and around in circles. Easy to tell by the increased salt in the air whenever they headed back toward the port. Since there seemed little point to this precaution if their destination was escape-proof, this gave Jethro hope.

"Hope you don't mind all the questions about sanitation," Jethro appeased, trying to sound like someone who didn't realize that so many organs would be taken that post-surgical infection would be a moot point.

The other man shook his head, distracted by the need to go single file to squeeze through a canyon of trash.

"You first," Jethro offered, trying to sound helpful. "You know the way."

The bum narrowed his eyes at Jethro, then shrugged and went first.

Jethro scanned the trash, looking for anything he could use later as a weapon. But he didn't spot anything before the trash canyon opened up, and the other man fell back in step beside him.

His kids. They could be losing their lives while this idiot went around in circles. Finally Jethro risked spooking the bum again. "Listen, I hope it isn't much farther. I don't have all day. Maybe someone else can get this done quicker. Maybe even pay more."

"Hold your horses, buddy," the man said with a jittery twitch of his lips that turned into an unconvincing smile.

Jethro wondered where this bum had gotten his archaic vocabulary.

The man narrowed his eyes again, scanning their surroundings. Twice.

Jethro scanned, too. Couldn't see any witnesses...

"Just about there, buddy. Hold tight." The bum about-faced, heading back through the canyon they'd just come through.

Falling behind again, Jethro made no comment, especially when he noticed— coming from this direction—a sharp plastic shard, which he quickly pocketed.

Shifty-eyed, the man hurried Jethro into a slight indentation in the trash behind one of the canyon walls. An upended tabletop turned out to be a door. Makeshift stairs took them under the garbage and into the basement of a nearby building.

Visual sweep...

Dog. Ten o'clock. German Shepherd. None of that cloned perfection. Big. Scarred. The real thing.

Bot. Two o'clock. No rubber ducky, or anything with pink or purple fur. It looked like it had been stolen from a construction site.

People. Twelve o'clock. Barely visible behind a cloudy, semi-transparent wall. Much farther away but lots of them. If all those people were staff, Jethro was in trouble. He tried to cover his nerves by asking the bum questions about a recovery room that he knew didn't exist.

They passed out of visual range of the dog and the bot. Closer now to the room full of people, Jethro could hear their voices, but couldn't make out their words. Then he heard his daughter's voice.

It must have shown on Jethro's face.

No mistaking the look on the bum's face as he watched Jethro, obviously putting two and two together, then snatched something out of his pocket.

The next thing Jethro knew, he had the man on the ground with the plastic shard he'd picked out of the garbage in the bum's jugular, which was now gushing blood. Jethro's other hand was over the man's mouth, silencing him.

Muscle memory...

Jethro took a gun out of the bum's hand and pocketed it along with the now-bloody plastic shard. Then he dragged the unconscious man out of sight behind some construction debris. Only problem was, Jethro had no idea what kind of gun he now had or what the hell it shot or even how to shoot it. SmartWeapons... What was Jethro supposed to do, think at it?

His daughter's voice again, upset but not yet hysterical. Even with his getting close and the door being ajar, he couldn't make out the words. With all those people in such a big room, somebody had to be staff. So Jethro fought off the all-but-irresistible urge to barge right in. Instead he circled around the semi-transparent walls of the room, looking for a way out the back of that basement that hopefully didn't include another bot and dog.

No bot and no dog, but no rear exit. Window?

Thickly packed and impassable trash visible outside. Probably no coincidence.

Nothing else inside except more construction debris, probably too heavy for them to have bothered moving.

Now his daughter's voice sounded hysterical. Jethro backtracked and bolted through the door.

Shabby waiting room filled with chairs. The good news was that most of the people looked like donors—apparently sedated and/or restrained—not staff. The bad news was the few that were not.

His daughter stood in the middle of the room, not restrained but dumbfounded at the sight of her dad.

Jethro's pig heart sank when he didn't see his son.

Behind his daughter a staff member crept forward with the light grace of a cat, despite weighing at least twice as much as the bum. Looking Jethro over, he crouched in a martial artist's stance, knees bent, presenting sideways. When their eyes met, they exchanged the unconscious nod of two martial artists recognizing each other.

Behind this man, two other staff members spread out, one advancing on the right, the other on the left.

His daughter bolted for the door behind Jethro and waited there.

Jethro charged the martial artist in the middle, feigning preparation for several standing martial-arts moves until close. Then Jethro dropped to one knee, slid under the man, hooked one arm around the man's thigh, and pushed him over sideways with the other.

But the man rolled with the agility of a cat, and his two fellow staff members now flanked Jethro.

Not knowing what else to do, Jethro pulled out the bum's gun. He waved it at all three as he sprang to his feet and hoped to hell that he held the gun correctly.

All three backed away, exchanging looks that Jethro hoped indicated their pay grade didn't justify unnecessary risks.

Jethro nodded toward some empty seats with restraints.

"No way!" spat out the flanker on the left.

"Kuso!" echoed the one on the right.

But what really made Jethro nervous was the hint of a smile he caught on the martial artist he'd taken down. Still, the man asked quietly, "That beauty the only stock you'll take? One martial artist to another?"

Jethro surveyed the waiting room. It looked like some of these people had been there for weeks. No, he didn't know any of the other donors, but he so ached to free them all. Still... Just a matter of time before someone or something spotted the bum's blood in the hallway—perhaps that construction-grade bot? Better to free one, his daughter, than none. He met the other martial artist's eyes. "Great roll, by the way, and...yeah, I'm kind of sweet on that little piece of ass."

The flankers smiled, convincing Jethro he'd gone in the right direction despite his internal cringe at saying such a thing about his daughter.

"Word of honor?" asked the martial artist.

Jethro, looking over the other donors again, didn't have to feign the heaviness he felt when he finally answered, "Word of honor."

They exchanged another brief nod before the three staff members headed for the empty seats. The martial artist started putting the other two in restraints.

"No," interrupted Jethro, nodding toward him. "You first."

Again that hint of a smile, which Jethro now interpreted as respect, before the martial artist let one of the flankers restrain him. Jethro watched how the flanker applied the restraints to both the martial artist and the other flanker. Then Jethro turned to see his daughter still behind him at the door. Motioning her over and handing her the gun, he approached the remaining flanker cautiously, careful not to get between the gun his daughter held and that flanker. But the last staff member even started his own restraints, making it easy for Jethro to finish the job. Using some old clothing he found on empty chairs, he gagged them all. And, even though he already knew the futility, looked around one last time for his son.

Then he looked up at his daughter. Shit, now what?

This time Jethro did it right, gently nudging the door open a sliver with his foot while hiding his daughter behind its not-at-all-transparent frame. No one visible to the left. He quickly stepped to the other side. No one visible to the right. No sound. He pulled his daughter into the hall.

His daughter still held the bum's gun. Jethro reached into his pocket to check the position of the plastic shard he'd taken out of the man's jugular. He was about to lead them around the bum's blood, so they wouldn't leave tracks on their way to the back—though he had no idea what they'd do when they got there.

Then he noticed wheel tracks in the blood, leading behind the construction debris where Jethro had hidden the bum's body.

Jethro pushed his daughter toward the front instead.

Silently panting, she mimed a dog.

Jethro indicated she should wait. Then he turned from his daughter and the front of the basement where he'd come in. On hands and knees, so his head wouldn't appear at the expected height, he peeked around the construction debris.

The construction-grade bot's full-disclosure screen was furiously scrolling through what looked like bargain-basement prices for black-market parts. The bot selected one for a liver, then carefully snapped and pushed aside some of the bum's ribs. A collector at its side had apparently already harvested both kidneys.

Jethro backed carefully, remembering how long he'd been waiting for his kids to return his calls from Boomers for the Stars. Had the need for harvested organs to be fresh, combined with a current dip in prices, at least saved his daughter?

The dog. It had to be now. Jethro mimed almost-drunken relaxation, hoping against hope the dog would let them pass if it didn't detect fear.

His daughter stuffed the gun into a pocket without having to be told. Yeah, a German Shepherd would probably react to that.

They headed toward the front, Jethro straining to hear the soft purr of wheels behind them and the sharp click of dog claws in front of them.

What he heard first was panting.

Couldn't hurry. Couldn't think about how useless the martial arts were against the reflexes of even a Chihuahua. Couldn't look back.

They passed the German Shepherd.

Behind them now... Jethro still heard panting.

They were getting close to the door.

The panting stopped.

Silence, except for their footsteps. Their breathing.

Then a low growl.

Jethro gauged distance, grabbed his daughter's hand, pushing her ahead of him, and ran for the door.

A clatter of dog claws hitting the floor, closing the distance between them way too fast. He should have kept walking despite the growl, waiting till the dog moved before he ran. What an idiot he'd been.

Jethro tried to position himself between the dog and his daughter, but she seemed to be fighting this and struggling with her clothes for some reason.

Jethro turned to face the dog.

The German Shepherd leaped for his throat, seeming to light up in some strange way Jethro didn't understand just before knocking him over. Why all the blood? He had yet to feel its teeth. In fact the dog felt...

Limp. Jethro pushed its bloody corpse aside.

"Sugoi!" His daughter, holding the bum's gun, pulled Jethro to his feet. Then she did something to the gun that turned it back off again and stuffed it back into her pocket.

"I'll never insult Japanese slang again," Jethro said softly, pushing her through the door as he spotted the construction-grade bot coming from the hall. They darted up the makeshift stairs, through the tabletop door, and out the back of the canyon of trash.

Now what?

Hide in the garbage? The dog could have found them, but with what senses was a construction-grade bot endowed?

While pulling his daughter around the canyon wall, he nodded toward the gun in her pocket. "Got the dog, but is it strong enough for that bot?"

She shook her head.

They both started burrowing into the opposite canyon wall. Just when Jethro thought they were reasonably well-concealed, he thought he heard the tabletop door opening, presumably the bot. But Jethro suddenly felt faint, perhaps from more physical exertion than even Archibald A. Astor could have prepared him for.

Kane kicked the panda at his feet yet again. Hidoi! If he didn't get out of this kuso office in this kuso nursing home soon, he'd go mad. Why hadn't he taken some other job, any other job, even hawking purple pugs at the airpad?

"I can understand your concern about extending credit," he purred into the phone. "It embarrasses me deeply to even ask for it. In fact it embarrasses me so deeply that I wouldn't ask if it was for just myself. But it's for the Boomers. We do very important work here, helping them, but that insta-freeze accident with the lab bot has shut down our whole operation. If you can just extend a little credit so I can get a new lab bot, it'll be no time before that grant money I was telling you about comes through and—"

Shimatta! How could koitsu, a syntho-hearted son of a clone if there ever was one, hang up on him? Kane went to kick Pink Panda again, but his toes were getting sore, and it hardly satisfied him anymore. He needed more.

He called up a new screen, 3D'd it and opened the colonel's file. The daughter. Something about that "next of kin." So what if, even in the current bad market, she'd probably been harvested by now? He found a full-body shot, enlarged it, and undid his pants. When his thoughts were the wildest, just before he came, he envisioned screwing her corpse, empty of all its major organs.

Phone. That rich client with more intel than anyone he knew. Shimatta! Kane had just made it.

"How's that heart treating you?" Kane asked, his own heart rate slowing gradually.

"Not reliable. Eeee? That information you gave me on the heart you sold me, the one now beating in my chest, was not reliable."

Kane's own heart rate started to climb again. Dealing with the "people in high places" wasn't all sugoi. "Eeee? I don't understand, but you know I'd do anything to help you, and−"

"The name of the donor? The one you promised was under thirty? The name you wouldn't give me? Wouldn't give me, the King of Intel on anyone or anything? Shimatta! I finally tracked it down myself and the only match is some Boomer aged−"

"That's what's 'not reliable'! How do you think I got you such a good price on a human heart? This is a nursing home; of course I swapped records so it would look like the heart came from some Boomer jiji!"

"But I don't understand how that would help—"

"You don't have to. That's my business, not yours. All you need to know is that you now have the heart of a perfectly healthy man under thirty in your chest and can do all the extreme sports you want. My word of honor."

"Not reliable."

"'Not reliable'?" Boomer-hearted son of a clone! And at least the first part of that curse was accurate. Kane had to catch his breath before he could continue in his usual, soft-spoken, conciliatory tone. "Well, well, we're old friends. No trade secrets, ne? If you really want all the boring details..."

"I want the name of the actual donor, ne?"

Kuso! Kane should never have panicked and permanently damaged that panda bot, fearing the "people in high places" wouldn't come through for him and protect him from the escaped colonel's testimony.

With no lab bot, how could he fake an "authentic" donor report for Mr. Not Reliable? But he collected himself, thinking this adversary just had to know more than he was telling, too. So Kane answered with his own request, "And I want to know a whole lot more from you, the 'King of Intel,' about Archibald A. Astor."

Mary's eyes snapped open. She was lying on a low bed, her face close to an elegant silk wall with five white cranes that were escaping from a bamboo thicket painted on it. She straightened her legs, and a plush cuddle-wrap readjusted itself, wrapping around her legs' new position and tucking under her toes.

Mary rolled over to her other side, turning away from the wall while the cuddle-wrap adjusted itself accordingly.

She could smell the room's thick cedar beams. A water fountain trickled over stones in one corner. The few other furnishings looked like priceless Japanese antiques.

Marilyn Monroe. Napoleon Bonaparte. Brooklyn. Mary remembered she had to help the people still in the nursing home and sprang to her feet.

Where was the woman with the lyrical voice? Or the red-headed "AAA"? Had anyone done anything about Boomers for the Stars?

Through the windows the sun was just beginning to set. How long had she been out? A day? A week?

The lacquered chest across the room... Wasn't that a little public phone on top of it? Mary bolted over the floor's tatami mats, snatched the phone off the chest, and sat cross-legged on the rush-covered straw.

The public phone forced her to endure a totally bogus ad for time travel before projecting the screen she had requested. Mary scrolled furiously, finally finding the correct regulatory agency for all nursing home abuse.

The pre-recorded stuff was smooth, obviously adeptly designed to calm the unnecessarily hysterical Boomer. The same quiet, calm voice, accompanied by music and soothing pictures, guided Mary through a million old-fashioned menus. But suddenly, when she first mentioned Boomers for the Stars, the music and images vanished. A very different voice, poorly recorded, said she was being transferred. She immediately recognized the next voice...a live human identifying himself as "Regulatory Agent Ronald Smith" and assuring her that her identity would never be revealed to anyone working for Boomers for the Stars.

It was Kane.

Without a word, Mary hung up. The phone's screen vanished. Had she been on video? She didn't remember any indication on the screen whether or not she had been.

The phone's screen blinked back to life to inform her, per African law, that the recipient of the last call was exercising the right to GPS-track an incoming call.

Mary dropped the phone as if it burnt her hand and ran out the door in her bare feet.

At the darker end of a hall Mary had never seen before, she did recognize another dilating door—like the one that had led to the spiral staircase and the room full of screens. Mary started for it, but then she heard voices.

At the other end of the hall, lit by the setting sun, the woman and the man from the screen room were squinting against the sunset, apparently searching a balcony.

"He's always out here this time of day," she said.

"That's what you said last time. Not reliable," he said.

"Why do you all of a sudden want him so urgently anyway? That look on your face... Did you just sell him out to Big Pharma?"

"No," the man said slowly. "I can promise you it's not that."

Instinct told Mary her best option was the dilating door. But she fought it down with her mother's mantra. She needed people. She should always rely on others.

These people were some of the very few rich and powerful left. They'd know what to do.

"I need your help!" Mary called out.

"The other one he wanted, on her feet!" Surprisingly it was the man, who'd shown little interest in her before, rushing to Mary's side while he put a phone to his ear. He placed a call, close enough now that Mary could just make out the "hello" on the other end, then asked, "Kane?"

Mary bolted for the dilating door.

"Hang on, Kane, this shouldn't be hard for me any longer."

The man pushed through the door behind her. Mary clattered down the stairs, the man clattering right behind her. Tears smarted. There was no way she could outrun this bastard. He wrapped both arms around her waist and literally snatched her off her feet on the lower floor's landing.

Then he straddled her, but he suddenly grimaced, a hand to his heart.

Mary rolled away. Half crawling and half on her feet, she started through the lower floor's dilating door.

A hand grabbed her ankle.

Mary managed to shake it off and get through the door. She could hear it dilate shut behind her. Then she could hear something banging against it, but it sounded muffled, like it was coming from the other side.

This new floor Mary hadn't seen before sported women dressed for evening in dull-colored asymmetrical clothes, which glittered softly. They all wore the same black hat the woman with the lyrical voice wore. The men all wore gray.

Mary leaped to her bare feet, realizing how much she must stand out in a simple white nightgown.

A woman passing looked her up and down. "The 'great unwashed.' How do they find their way in here?"

"Security," answered the man with her. "So very few of us left and they can't protect us? Don't know why we even pay these people."

Mary darted for the closest turn in the hall. People screamed or tsked in her wake. Mary skidded around the corner, then peeked back around it at the dilating door she'd just come from.

No sign of the man pursuing her.

Did security cameras all over this more-public hall mean he no longer had to keep up with her physically?

Mary searched the wallpaper, tastefully holographed with forests of bamboo undulating in a nonexistent breeze.

Couldn't tell.

Elevators, a long way off, beckoned at the other end of this new hall.

But Mary ran to the closest door, all but invisible amidst the bamboo, and barreled through it

Behind it was a sloppy jumble of open screens, a sleek silver bot lying on the floor—no furry animals here—and a man with his back to her, not in formal grays.

"No one's allowed in here," he said without turning around. "Especially barefoot people in nightgowns." He still hadn't turned around.

Mary realized the screens the man struggled with covered the hallways on that floor. Maybe the silver bot lying on its side—obviously malfunctioning since it showed no full-disclosure screen—monitored the hall screens ordinarily. Odd that the hall screens didn't just monitor themselves, but no time to question that.

She checked the screens. Still no sign of the man pursuing her. She backed out of the door and ran for the elevators. Was the man pursuing her seeing empty screens while the man in the room she'd just left sorted out the silver-bot

249

malfunction? Would she still be traceable in the elevator? No way to tell either. Mary all but crashed into the wall next to the elevators and pushed an antique-looking call button.

People passed.

Time passed.

Mary rolled her eyes and stamped her bare feet on the cool, hard floor.

"...if we could just find that cheap bot he got at the airpad."

The woman with the lyrical voice! Mary looked everywhere, but all the women were wearing the same hat.

Finally she heard the elevator doors open behind her and backed in, colliding with something rock-hard.

"Please be advised that I'm directly behind you. Injury could result from..."

Mary tuned out what turned out to be another sleek silver bot and hit the button for the lobby.

Till the bot got out, she watched its full-disclosure screen. Its only concerns consisted of importing expensive non-essentials for the very few people still living in Africa who could afford them. It had apparently not been informed that it should be on the lookout for a barefoot derelict in a white nightgown.

After the bot got out, the elevator dived for the lobby, but it felt like Mary's stomach had been left behind.

Lobby. The dark startled her. She tripped over some debris and heard some rodent squeal. Obviously the people upstairs never came here. Probably only bots, oblivious to its condition. Mary could feel the filth with her bare feet.

Frantic, she tried to find that foyer she remembered from coming up, but—as soon as she walked far enough away from the elevator she'd come down on—all light vanished. Lost in an endless maze of broken elevators, she cut her foot on something in the debris. But then some instinct made her stop, even her breathing.

Muffled. So barely audible she couldn't be sure it wasn't just wishful thinking. But there it was again, rhythmic and slow.

She ran down a hall one way and held her breath.

Nothing.

She ran down the hall the other way.

Nothing.

She came back to the center again and took a different hallway.

There it was again, rhythmic and slow.

Finally she turned the correct corner, and saw the light of Mr. Cocoa Puffs' broken-elevator bedroom.

Mary remembered the woman with the lyrical voice's words, "...if we could just find that cheap bot he got at the airpad."

But she'd need to hack into it.

Then she remembered Mr. Cocoa Puffs' words, "This baby could hack into anything from a bot to a C-2 launcher."

Mary thought of "Marilyn Monroe" and "Napoleon Bonaparte" back at the nursing home without any idea who they really were or what fate Boomers for the Stars had in store for them.

Then she slipped past the elevator door trying unsuccessfully to close off Mr. Cocoa Puffs' makeshift bedroom and stole his second snarl of wires with alligator clips.

Jethro's eyes snapped open. His daughter. That construction-grade bot. The first thing he saw was his daughter looking at him, obviously in agony.

But, he couldn't help it, his eyes closed again.

When Jethro's eyes opened the next time his daughter was still looking at him, but...she was smiling. "Sugoi, Dad, I was so worried. But it's that stuff you were given. First you vomit, then sometime later there's a comatose period..."

But his eyes closed again.

The next time Jethro's eyes opened he tried to talk.

"Don't worry, Dad, you're safe. That bot didn't find us. Everything's fine, in fact more than fine. I've just had it proven to me that my brother got away!"

He realized the jerking around his mouth was a weak attempt at a huge smile and didn't fight his eyes closing again.

Sometime later, eyes still closed, he became aware of his daughter's voice again.

"...so I really have to apologize for ever doubting you! You were great! Sugoi! And I can't thank you enough for all you did!"

Such sweet, sweet words. This daughter, finally, fully recognizing him. Almost worth the nightmare they'd been through.

"And he'll be so excited..."

Who would be excited? His son, who she said before was safe? But why did his daughter's voice sound...flirty, like it had when she was talking to Brooklyn in Boomers for the...

"...when he learns he really will be going to the stars!"

Jethro opened his eyes.

His daughter was leaning over him, but not looking at him any longer—clearly flirting with someone instead.

Leaning over Jethro from the other side, now reaching a hand out to caress his daughter's cheek, was Kane.

"Dad! You're awake! Don't look stricken; I told you everything was okay. I called Boomers for the Stars, that wonderful place that got you out of your wheelchair, and Kane here rushed right over to save us both from those horrible organ harvesters in the garbage."

"Careful," said Kane, putting an arm around Jethro's daughter. "I recognize that look on your father's face; I've seen it before. I know your father's generally lucid, but sometimes our star travelers experience an unfortunate period of confusion when they're coming out of the comatose stage. Typically it manifests in a rather alarming degree of totally irrational paranoia."

Jethro grabbed his daughter's hand, still struggling to speak. Finally he managed, "Run!"

Kane pulled his daughter away. "See what I mean?" He signaled a new bot, this one a sleek silver model, then pushed Jethro's daughter out of the room, saying, "It's better you don't witness this."

Once the door closed behind her, there was no mistaking the look on Kane's face when he returned his attention to Jethro. It wasn't friendly.

Jethro found his voice. "I won't fight you this time, Kane. I'll even back you, telling her goodbye with a big smile before I 'head for the stars' after recovering from that little bout of 'paranoia.' You...you're interested in her, I could see that. She'd make a great wi— Girlfriend or whatever. And she doesn't know! She doesn't suspect a thing! If you should ever run into legal trouble, she could bear witness to the impeccable ethics of Boomers for the Stars."

Judging from the hint of a smile throughout his speech, Kane was enjoying watching Jethro squirm.

Jethro swallowed hard. "Look, I don't know why you do what you do. Maybe you...have your reasons. But somewhere at

some time you must have had a...
Syntho?"

"Never," Kane said with scorn.

"Pig?"

"No."

"Chimp?"

Kane shook his head. "100% human."

Jethro's turn to smirk. Human, of course. He'd been to Vietnam. No other animal could be as heartless. But Jethro had no choice; he had to try.

"Organ prices took a recent nosedive anyway. Sometime, somehow, you may look back on all this...with at least a question if not remorse. You can at least wipe your conscience clean on my account if you just let my daughter live. Promise me." It took every ounce of willpower Jethro had to say the next word to this human-hearted monster. "Please."

But Jethro could see he was starting to lose Kane's attention as the man typed away on his shiny new bot.

Jethro stared across the lab at the insta-freeze he'd pushed Pink Panda into what seemed like years ago. But he wasn't really seeing it. He was seeing something he swore he'd never let back into conscious memory again. And it wasn't Vietnam.

"Kane, I was a pig when I first got this pig heart. I had a beautiful wife, a beautiful daughter, a son, and four grandchildren, all full-grown. But I'd always loved fast cars, ever since I was a kid. And when they first came out with those crazy-fast hydrogen carts... In the accident that put me in that wheelchair I lost much more than the use of my legs. All eight of us were in that cart. I was drag racing a flyer overhead. I was the only one who survived."

Kane, typing into the silver bot, said nothing.

"I could never bear to remarry. But I finally rented delivery bots and implanted my sperm in them. My new son..."

Kane looked up for a moment, obviously thinking of something else, but happening to look at Jethro.

"My new son who escaped the organ harvesters..."

Kane seemed to see Jethro for a moment and nod agreement without even realizing he was doing it. Then he returned to his typing.

"...and this new daughter are all I have left."

Silence. More typing. "Shimatta!"

Jethro directed his attention to the silver bot's full-disclosure screen. Graphs showing kidney prices had taken yet another sharp dive down. More typing. Map of Boomers for the Stars showing Rubber Ducky ushering what Jethro assumed was his daughter out the front door. Jethro fought the urge to try and run after her and ask her to confirm that Kane had proven to her that his son was okay. Then he remembered his daughter flirting with Kane, and his pig heart sank. How much "proof" would be necessary to convince a silly girl?

At least, for now, her silliness was keeping her safe.

Kane waved in Jethro's direction, speaking to the silver bot. "Get koitsu out of here for now. Back in the dayroom."

"To talk to the others?" Jethro had blurted it out without thinking.

Kane finally focused his full attention on Jethro.

Jethro's pig heart froze. Somehow, looking into Kane's eyes, he knew all the others were gone. Marilyn, Napoleon, and, yes, he grieved for Brooklyn, too. Jethro had deserted them, and now they were gone. First his entire family. Now... Jethro's stomach seized.

"Only one other patient just now," put in Kane, strangely. "You should get a kick out of this one, Colonel. Abraham Lincoln? Michael Jordan? Rory Randall? Jesus Christ? No, this one thinks he's Archibald A. Astor!"

But now that Kane finally deigned to talk to him, Jethro hardly listened. Marilyn. Napoleon. Brooklyn. Even the shiny new silver bot approaching didn't seem so shiny and new close up. Jethro even thought he detected its full-disclosure screen flickering. Still, the fighter in him noted the solid construction which certainly left Pink Panda in the dust, and the law-enforcement-grade handcuff attachments it used on Jethro.

Jethro looked down as his own hands, now those of a young man—the young man he had once been. But it did no good. He'd lived so long. All the Archibald A. Astor— How had Kane known he knew that name anyway? Had Jethro been babbling while he was unconscious? Anyway all the vials in the world, all the new hearts and livers and who-knew-what-else couldn't put Humpty Dumpty back together again. He'd seen too much and, yes, done far too much for far too many decades that he could never forgive himself for.

Jethro's vision blurred, but that silver bot's handcuffs kept him from wiping his eyes until he was released into the dayroom. There he sniffled his way past the wallpaper with the old masters' portraits that were supposed to follow a person walking by with their eyes. It somehow seemed appropriate now, even fitting, that all he saw in those eyes that were supposed to be following him was the vacuous emptiness of old television static. When he couldn't take the pain of it all any longer he looked down at the floor, listlessly following the faulty programming that depressed his footsteps in the shag carpeting before he got there. But the ever-changing colors were giving him a headache.

He felt a hand on his shoulder. Jethro turned toward it like a starving man at the scent of food, hoping against hope that the next thing he'd hear would be, "Wasup, B?"

But it wasn't Brooklyn; the hand couldn't have been whiter. What Jethro heard instead was, "It's just paranoia, a side effect I unfortunately didn't anticipate since none of my research indicated the slightest chance of it. But it'll pass. Eventually our team of professionals will have you right as rain."

Oh yeah. Thinks he's Archibald A. Astor. Kane must have covered his tracks by spinning the same paranoia yarn for "AAA" that he did for Jethro's daughter.

Jethro trudged on past Rubber Ducky. Was he projecting how he was feeling about everything, including himself, or did Rubber Ducky look surprisingly old, beat-up, and run down now?

Up ahead: the cuddle couch. Where was JFK, or Marilyn, interrupting with her breathy queries about where JFK was? Or Napoleon, endlessly blaming Waterloo on anyone and everyone except himself?

Jethro sank into the cuddle couch, letting it jiggle him with its caresses while he sobbed.

That hand on his shoulder again. "What have I done to you?"

"No," said Jethro. "It's what I've done to myself, spending decade after weary decade tricking myself into believing I was a good person because of what I did a very long time ago for a few short years—under extraordinary and completely unusual and atypical conditions—in Vietnam."

"Introspection. It leads us all to the same kind of conclusion. You are not alone. You are not unusual." The other's man's voice was rich with compassion.

This really was a good person! Jethro was so moved that he clapped a hand over this "AAA's" hand, still on Jethro's shoulder. Who was he really? Could Jethro—somehow—manage to get him one of the real AAA's vials so he could rediscover himself? More to the point, could Jethro, who had lost so many people and screwed up so much, get this "AAA" safely out of Boomers for the Stars?

Jethro turned to look up at the other man, far younger than he'd imagined. "AAA" had a slow but infectious grin that was spreading over a face with freckles that matched his flaming red hair.

SUE HOLLISTER BARR

Kane was on the phone again. Same annoying bit. Hidoi! He was getting so sick of saying the same stupid kuso over and over again. "Look, even people under thirty can have minor heart attacks. You're still alive, screaming at me, ne?"

"Not reliable! My heart came from someone with a history of what...rheumatic fever? How long does it take for you to get me the *real* donor's name?"

"Speaking of 'not reliable,' how long will it take you to get me the history on the silver bot you gave me in exchange for my setting aside all my remaining AAA vials for your chemical analysis? That silver bot's full-disclosure screen keeps blinking out."

It went on. Never mind that Kane's remaining AAA vials were missing. Dasai! While Mr. Extreme Sports yelled, Kane stared at the safe to search it again. Would it open this time or not? But, to be fair, there was only one time it hadn't opened, the day that Brooklyn with the hacker history had gotten through the security door and‒ Kuso! And Kane had later found stuff missing!

The safe opened. Kane scrambled to locate his money stash. Double kuso! The money was gone, too!

Kane played the trump card he'd been saving. "So with all the security back-ups you have in 'high places' you couldn't‒even with your little episode, which probably wasn't a heart attack anyway‒catch my Star Captain Mary?"

There was a long pause. "I have to go."

Kane clenched his fist. Shame he didn't have Pink Panda around to kick anymore.

But of the three people Kane had asked Mr. Extreme Sports—with all his power and intel—to track down and deliver, Star Captain Mary and even that jiji colonel weren't the most important. The real, genuine Archibald A. Astor was a pleasant surprise and far more valuable. Sugoi! Remarkable that Mr. Extreme Sports had fallen for Kane's convoluted lie about needing AAA to undo the locks on the remaining vials. Must have been distracted, worrying—as well he should be—about his heart.

Kane had already gotten out of AAA that, amazingly, that cheap little purple-pug bot contained the results of an entire lifetime of brilliant research. Most of it, breakthroughs in interstellar travel and colonization, Kane had no personal use for. But the purple pug had the formula for that fountain-of-youth stuff in the missing vials that Kane wanted so badly.

273

And—rakki!—AAA had even mentioned an odd byproduct he was studying that appeared to have the opposite effect, causing severe and apparently equally irreversible dementia. Perfect way to control the next colonel who wandered into Boomers for the Stars.

If Kane could just keep up the ruse of being AAA's trusted colleague a little longer, he should have everything he needed from him. And that shouldn't be hard, given the man's really pathological naiveté. With any luck, parts prices would have risen by then, and Kane could then harvest the colonel and AAA together. Mr. Extreme Sports—in fact anyone who'd ever met AAA—would easily believe that the trusting fool had wandered off and been eaten by lion clones. It was all so sugoi!

That jiji colonel had thought Kane wasn't listening to all that self-indulgent kuso about his life. But he was wrong. Kane had listened. And, he, Kane was going to ensure that he reached the colonel's age without any regrets at all. No more stupid moves. No more stupid assumptions about anybody or anything else being reliable.

None of the rest of them mattered. If he had to, Kane would harvest each and every one, even that cute daughter of the colonel's. After he had a little fun with her.

But with all that valuable-to-humanity stuff Kane was going to get out of AAA, and/or his pug, before plucking out his kidneys? Kane was going to have the only things that mattered: a very long life and all the money in the world.

Mary squinted toward the sun, struggling over the garbage-strewn landscape in bare feet that now bled.

She had to find that purple bot of AAA's. She had to save Marilyn, Napoleon, and Brooklyn. She figured all three would have to have their wits about them, or she'd never get them out of Boomers for the Stars. So she needed more AAA vials for Marilyn and Napoleon.

Finally she looked sideways, having found what she was looking for, the swarm of garbage-dwellers waiting beneath the high windows for leftover food. With this starting point and the sun to guide her, she should be able to find the next landmark on the way to that purple pug, the upturned chassis of the faux 1956 Thunderbird.

Mary kept the sun to her back now as she hurried between the two silk buildings, struggling over the now-deserted trash.

She thought she heard something, which she shouldn't with everyone beneath the windows to catch the food. A cloned lion?

Mary pushed on, thought she heard it again, and turned to check behind her.

But, squinting into the sun, she was hardly able to see.

Then she heard the clanging, ridiculously loud announcement: "Authentic Archibald A. Astor's..." Pause. "...best liquid self-adjusting sunglasses on Earth. Guaranteed you'll never be bothered by the sun's glare again or your money back."

Mary smiled, so fixated on finding the purple pug and relieved that what she'd heard wasn't a cloned lion that she didn't really focus on what had just found her. Instead she steadied herself with one hand on the half-disassembled sales bot and plucked something that had gotten stuck in one of her bleeding feet out with the other. Then she caressed the bot's old-fashioned, two-dimensional sign projector. "Trying for a repeat sale?"

"Authentic Archibald A. Astor's..." came the clanging announcement again. "...best liquid repeat-sale attractor on Earth. Guaranteed you'll never want for repeat sales or your money back."

Mary petted the broken old bot fondly, shaking her head before pulling away to rush on. Then she came to her senses. Duh! Maybe she didn't need to find that purple pug. "Got any more of that authentic Archibald A. Astor's best liquid elderly tune-up on Earth?"

The bot paused, seemed to be scanning her, then whirred a bit. Mary figured she could literally hear it thinking. Finally the clanging voice announced,

"You have no need for that." Pause. "Authentic Archibald A. Astor's best liquid repeat-sale attractor—"

Mary tuned out the rest to curse silently and wonder what idiot programmed a sales bot to question a potential sale, even if it was a repeat sale.

She looked back at the now-silent bot. Did it always pitch in response to its customers' verbally stated needs? Should she talk about feeling confused again, or would that even work now that it had scanned her? Or was it some genius who had programmed it not to sell the same item to the same person so they couldn't use it to prove fraud since none of it was supposed to work? Then it hit her. Liquid. Every sales pitch she'd ever heard out of it included Archibald A. Astor and liquid.

All the same stuff it had sold her? All that one type of vial it must have stolen off a cart headed for Boomers for the Stars? Just a wild, stupid fluke that it actually did what the bot said it would when it sold a vial to her?

Mary spoke. "Authentic Archibald A. Astor's best liquid repeat-sale attractor on Earth. That's something I need. Two vials, please, one for me and one for...my sales partner."

"Authentic Archibald A. Astor's best liquid repeat-sale attractor on Earth. Two vials left. Eighty each." The bot had its money receiver extended.

Money. Mary didn't have any.

"Show me the two vials first. I want to be sure the vials are of good quality."

A picture of two vials, identical to the one she'd bought, appeared on its old-fashioned, two-dimensional sign projector.

"No, the actual vials."

A little door slid open on its chest. The glass behind it was cracked and dirty but she could just barely make out two Archibald A. Astor vials behind it.

The door started to close.

Mary dug the fingernails of one hand under the edge of the door, trying to stop it from closing. She dug the fingernails of the other hand under the cracks in the glass, cutting her fingertips.

SUE HOLLISTER BARR

"Unauthorized procurement of unpaid-for merchandise is strictly prohibited by law." The bot seemed to be replacing its money-receiver attachment with something not-as-yet-visible.

Mary put her fist through the glass, grabbing the vials, just as pins punctured her, hitting all the major nerves closest to her skin. BadAcu. The pain was unendurable—exactly what one would expect from bad acupuncture—but she ran through the garbage anyway, listening to the bot's siren alarm behind her and clutching the vials. Until she felt them crumble in her hand.

What? The bot's siren was far enough behind her. Mary stopped, furiously plucking the BadAcu pins out as she looked down at the vials.

There was no sign that any liquid had been in them for a long time. The tops were missing, and the insides were dusty. At least she didn't hear the siren anymore, although Mary heard something behind her.

"Authentic Archibald A. Astor's..." Pause. "...best liquid pain reliever—"

"Sorry about your glass window," Mary interrupted before moving on, looking for that T-bird.

BadAcu's claims had been correct: What had been unendurable pain did recede quickly once she'd plucked out the last pin. But that just meant the agony in her feet it had been masking resurfaced.

Mary trudged on. How hard could it be to spot a car upended in the trash?

People. She could hear them behind her now, returning from the food windows. Someone passed, and Mary caught a whiff of some expensive, imported cheese. Her stomach rumbled. She looked forward again and caught a blinding glint in the setting sun of something above the usual trash height.

The T-bird.

Once abreast of it she started looking in the trash for anything that would spark a memory of having come that way before, but the light was failing fast.

Mary was starved. Her feet were killing her. The light was almost gone. She stepped on something furry, but only yanked a faux-fur jacket out of the trash. Still, she kept it, not knowing where she'd be sleeping. She stepped on something that wiggled, but it wasn't a small bot, it was a small live something—Mary didn't even know what—that bit her ankle before scurrying away. Finally she stepped on something that hurt like hell, with lots of pointy edges, but lit up. She picked up a broken porta-light. That helped a bit.

At last she found the bot. Mary collapsed next to it.

No visible full-disclosure screen.

Mary jiggled it.

Nothing.

Groaning, Mary dragged herself back to her feet. Yawning, she walked around to the other side of it, the side closer to Boomers for the Stars. From there she tried to step on its skin folds from the same angle she'd stepped on them the first time.

It wiggled. Its full-disclosure screen half flickered to life. It identified its owner's full name as Andrew A. Adams. She didn't know why he'd used his real name instead of Archibald A. Astor for the bot...perhaps because the bot required ID? But it didn't matter.

Mary propped the porta-light up in the surrounding garbage and set to work with the alligator-clipped cables she'd stolen from Mr. Cocoa Puffs' elevator bedroom.

But the porta-light was now dimming, needing a solar re-charge that wouldn't be available for hours. And Mary had no real knowledge of what she was doing. Her only reward for her endless attempts to hack into the bot was hearing its endless lectures about how illegal that was.

Once its screen revealed it was 4:23 a.m. Mary caught herself nodding many times.

Finally she curled up to put her head down on the faux-fur jacket she'd found for "just a minute."

The next time Mary's eyes opened it was full day. She'd heard something. She sat up with a start, then felt a hand on her shoulder.

"Wasup, B? Didst thou first find the pug?"

Mary turned to look up at Brooklyn, who held what looked like a GPS made of garbage scraps in his other hand. He was flanked by Marilyn and Napoleon, but somehow they didn't look like Marilyn Monroe and Napoleon Bonaparte.

Mary was on her feet, wreathed with smiles, then choked with tears of gratitude. She wrapped her arms around all three.

"My dear girl, your feet!" That cultured woman's voice had come from...Marilyn Monroe?

Mary stepped back in confusion.

"Marilyn" winked at her. "Allow me to introduce myself. My name is Catherine."

Mary beamed, mimicking Catherine's speech a bit. "I am absolutely delighted to meet you!"

Catherine turned to "Napoleon." "And this lovely gentleman is Philippe, an avid Francophile and student of warfare if there ever was one."

"*Enchanté!*" Philippe's voice was much deeper than "Napoleon's."

"But those feet, dear girl!" Catherine gestured—elegantly—for Mary to sit so Catherine could look at them.

Brooklyn held up Mr. Cocoa Puffs' alligator-clipped cables. "From whence came these?"

"I stole them," Mary answered.

"O, she doth teach the torches to burn bright!" cried Brooklyn, grinning at

Mary and swinging the cables about in triumph.

Jethro reviewed all he knew about Boomers for the Stars' weaknesses and strengths for the umpteenth time. In his mind he envisioned the exact layout, Rubber Ducky's top speed, different trajectories for getting to the front door, and the time it would take "AAA" to run across the lawn to the weakness in the fence while Jethro did his damnedest to hold off that silver bot. But Jethro knew the real challenge to getting "AAA" safely out of Boomers for the Stars was sitting right in front of him. It was "AAA" himself.

Just now the freckled redhead was furiously scrolling through "his" latest research on Rubber Ducky's full-disclosure screen. How could Jethro convince him that it wasn't paranoia that prompted

Jethro's warnings against Kane? He decided to try a different ploy...

"So, any memories of your childhood...of anyone ever calling you Archibald?"

"Andy, not Archibald."

Bingo! Why hadn't Jethro tried this to show "AAA" he wasn't really "AAA" before? "So, you're not really Archibald A. Astor?"

"No, I'm not." Andy stopped scrolling to look up at Jethro. "I'm sorry. I should have told you before, my friend. It's the least you deserve, a simple thing really, my real name."

"What is it?"

"Andrew A. Adams."

Still the AAA-bit? Red hair... Of course it could easily be colored, and all sorts of things were possible with the extensive cosmetic work Jethro assumed this guy had had, but he really did look too young for the classic Boomer identity-confusion bit. Still Jethro pushed that aside and did the mental equivalent of crossing his fingers before asking his next question.

"So, you're not really researching a fountain of youth?"

Andy was back to scrolling. "Just the opposite. An odd byproduct that appears to have the exact opposite effect, causing dementia and typical Boomer identity disassociation."

Jethro mentally crossed both fingers and toes before asking, "Byproduct of what?"

"The fountain of youth of mine you took."

Still thinks he's AAA! Jethro sagged back into the cuddle couch, defeated, then jerked back out of it, annoyed when it started cuddling him. Back to the drawing board. "And you trust Kane with all this because...?"

"The people who rescued me from the riffraff after I left the airpad told me that I could trust him implicitly."

"And you trust them because...?"

Andy turned away from his scrolling and joined Jethro on the cuddle couch. When it tried to cuddle them both, and they both swatted it back, they shared a laugh.

"Look," started Andy softly. "I'll admit I can be gullible, overly trusting. All I've ever wanted was to help people, including saving them from the extinction being trapped on this planet will soon bring by making it really possible for them to survive among the stars. So maybe I can't bear to think they're not worth the time and trouble I've put into saving them."

Jethro was both touched and horrified. Okay, he'd watched "JFK" do a damn convincing JFK. And "Marilyn," despite an almost ludicrous failure to live up to the part physically, did a perfectly adequate Marilyn Monroe. But Andy, whatever his real name was... Somehow... Something about him topped them all. Every bone in Jethro's body told him that talking him out of his AAA persona was hopeless. So Jethro was going to have to find a way to talk him out of trusting Kane as if he really were AAA. "So, knowing this about yourself, you should know to be more cautious than you think is actually justified."

"A reasonable point," Andy said, thinning his lips in apparent recognition of what Jethro had said, "but not in this case."

"Why?"

"Because both the people who saved me after I arrived in Africa and Kane, if they weren't trustworthy, could have already made a fortune handing Big Pharma my head on a silver platter."

"Not necessarily," said Jethro, remembering all the Machiavellian maneuvering he'd had to survive to become colonel. He squared himself off in front of Andy, ignoring the cuddle couch's renewed efforts. "I beg you to listen to me. Many is the man who's lost everything, up to and including his life, because he didn't see another's less obvious, secondary agenda."

Was it wishful thinking, or did Jethro at last see the dawning of a new consciousness, a new way of looking at things, in Andy's blue eyes?

The sound of the security door to Kane's domain opening.

Jethro looked away from Andy to see both the new silver bot and Kane, eyes squinted as he looked at Jethro and Andy together on the cuddle couch.

Jethro realized in horror that Kane would have to be an idiot not to pick up on the suspicious intensity of their conversation.

"Ah, my beloved colleague," said Kane, "what impeccable bedside manner. Stunning for a top scientist."

Andy looked up at Kane.

Jethro watched Andy like a hawk, alert to even the slightest change in his demeanor, the teeniest evidence that he no longer took Kane at face value.

But there was none. The grin that spread over Andy's freckled face at the sight of Kane was totally ingenuous. It was also so infectious and full of boyish charm that it was all Jethro could do to resist grinning himself, until a sharp tug at his gut reminded him of what was to come.

Andy leapt to his feet with eyes that were only for Kane, giving the apparently all-but-forgotten Jethro a patronizing pat on the knee. "I've made some stunning leaps in getting my research notes up-to-date so it'll all make sense to you," he told Kane brightly. "I am, as it were, making splendid progress in..." He paused to pat Rubber Ducky and wink impishly at Kane, "getting all my ducks in order."

Jethro collapsed in defeat into the back of the cuddle couch that immediately started jostling him around. But he no longer cared. Helpless, he watched in horror as Andy wrapped an arm around Kane and hurried him back towards the security door that led to the lab, blabbing something about, "I can't wait to show you!" Even the glitch in the shag-carpet programming that depressed itself for his footsteps prior to Andy's arrival seemed to reflect Andy's innocent, boyish glee.

The security door closed behind them. Jethro sprang out of the cuddle couch, but only to pace the dayroom, watching all the eyes in the portraits mark his passing with nothing more than television static.

Rubber Ducky got in his way, presenting a full-disclosure screen full of choices for Jethro's next meal.

Jethro smirked. Whatever all else, the food at Boomers for the Stars had always been quite good. But he waved Rubber Ducky away, even when it repeatedly tried to take his order. Even though he was starved.

Hours later, Jethro was surprised to see Kane come through the security door without his new toy, and it must have shown.

"My new bot's a little busy right now," said Kane with a smile. "Prices for kidneys have finally gone up."

Kane chuckled, once he was back in his office, remembering the look on the colonel's face when Kane intimated the silver bot was already harvesting Andy's kidneys. Jiji! Least the colonel deserved after causing him so much trouble. Shame, though, that kidney prices hadn't really gone up...

Kane returned his attention to the screens floating around in front of him, kicking the "new" silver bot generating them when they all, even its full-disclosure screen, flickered off again. Still it was a lot more powerful than Rubber Ducky. And at least it was originally a top-tier security bot. That should take care of any further escape attempts by the colonel, ne?

All the screens flickered back on.

Andy returned after a long time from doing something in the lab. He started waxing poetic yet again about how his research should make interstellar colonization a reality, then looked at Kane strangely. "That won't upset you, will it? Losing the revenue from sending Boomers to the stars as guinea pigs?"

Kane darted a look at the safe. "No, of course not. Any loss of mere money is worth helping all of humanity in such a way!" Then Kane spotted something new on a screen. "Look! I just found that homing device for your purple pug, so I can easily retrieve it for you...so we can save all of humanity together. Yabai! That's very useful, ne?" Kane found himself darting another look at the safe, thinking of all the money he could make selling Andy's research after he'd been harvested, then caught Andy looking at him even more strangely.

"By the way," Andy said slowly, "I came across something today that I told you wouldn't be available till we retrieve my pug, but I was wrong."

"Double yabai! What is it?"

Andy pulled a vial out of his pocket. "Fountain of Youth."

Kane looked at the fool who, especially after the pug-homing-device discovery, had just signed his own death warrant. Kidney prices be damned. With his own Fountain of Youth and that pug to sell—probably to those who stood to gain the most by suppressing Andy's research, like those really still sending Boomers to the stars—it would be worth harvesting Andy and the colonel just to get them safely out of the way.

Andy surprised him by pulling a chair so close that their knees touched as, still holding the vial, he faced Kane. Andy's voice throbbed with emotion. "Aside from my Fountain of Youth, all I ever wanted—ever since I was a little boy and first heard of the speedy death sentence staying on this planet has become—was to save humanity! Please understand that!"

"Oh, I do," said Kane, pulling his knees back a bit since the intensity combined with the physical contact somehow made him nervous. But, with that contact broken, Kane found his old voice. "And the reason I understand is because—shimatta!—that's all I've ever wanted. Why else would I devote my life to sending all these Boomers to the stars, hoping against hope that they'd find a planet we could have survived on without all your research? But the lifetime of brilliant work you miraculously crammed into—of all things— a cheap layover-airpad purple-pug bot? Sugoi! Together we'll keep it out of the hands of those so short-sighted they'd rather just make money in their own lifetime rather than save their own children and children's children. Together we'll take humanity to the stars!" Kane caught himself darting another look at the safe over Andy's shoulder, thinking about how much money he was going to make disregarding the useless lives of anyone who came after him.

Andy handed him the vial.

"Thank you, my friend and colleague! Allow me just a moment to put this in a safe place."

"You're not going to take it right now?" Andy seemed very upset by that.

"No, no, my welfare can wait," said Kane, patting Andy's shoulder as he got up. "Don't want to be puking all over you when we fetch that purple pug, ne? After all, what's more important, my health or saving humanity?"

Kane heard Andy getting up behind him, but not before Kane had typed what he needed to into the silver bot.

Kane wasn't going to take any chances with that one vial of Fountain of Youth. No stashing it in a safe that had already been hacked into, ne? He had, however, been truthful when he'd said he wasn't going to drink it right away—because of the initial bout of horrendous vomiting. Kane had to prioritize and make sure a few other important matters were taken care of first.

On his way through the office door to the lab, where he was planning to hide the vial, he glanced back over his shoulder briefly. He was gratified to see that one important matter had been resolved. Apparently that silver ex-security bot had done something to silence Andy from a distance. But Andy's mouth, which had been screaming, went slack now that his head had been removed. Shame about the kidneys that would now be worthless, but the prices were ridiculously low anyway.

Mary shuddered but then wrote it off as being for no reason and stretched out on her back, smiling up at the stars. Her feet that hardly hurt anymore were snugly encased in bandaging that the former Marilyn Monroe, now a most-elegant Catherine, had made for her. Philippe could be heard reciting poetry in French with that voice that was so much deeper than it had been when he thought he was Napoleon Bonaparte. Brooklyn occasionally interjected part of some

Shakespearean sonnet as he tended the shish kebobs he had skewered on pieces of scrap metal. They sizzled over a fire he'd made in a huge hydrogen-cart fender.

Occasionally a soft breeze teased Mary with the smoky scent of onions and some kind of meat. Remembering the rodents around the elevator banks and the thing she'd stepped on in the garbage that had bitten her ankle, Mary thought it best not to inquire into the particulars.

A gentle, elegant laugh at her side...

"What?" Mary asked.

"I'm remembering," Catherine said.

"Remembering being The Blonde Bombshell?"

"No, no. Long before those things I never did have in my life, like romantic love, led me to imagine myself, of all things in heaven and earth..." Catherine broke off to giggle like a very young and foolish girl this time.

Brooklyn contributed, "There are more things in heaven and earth, Horatio, than are dreamt of in your philosophy."

Catherine struggled to suppress her giggles and continued, voice full of wonder. "Marilyn Monroe!"

Mary shifted her weight on her makeshift bed. Metal scraped against metal far beneath her, reminding her that underneath the soft cushioning Catherine had shared with her was a garbage dump.

"What do you remember?" Catherine asked. "From before you were Star Captain Mary."

Mary looked deep into the jewel-like splendor of the night sky. "Mostly that I was never Star Captain Mary." The Southern Cross called to her. Beneath it was Centaurus, including the closest star, Proxima Centauri. Next to it was the constellation once known as Argo Navis, a great jewel-bedecked ship.

"So...you really did want to go to the stars?"

"It was all I ever wanted!"

"What happened?"

Suddenly tears threatened. "I came to Africa long before any of the great waves of immigration. For the space program. It was when they were still getting rid of the first generation that threatened to live forever, us Boomers, by throwing us at the stars."

"*Exactement!*" interjected Philippe, drawing close. Then he switched to English. "Appeased the bleeding hearts by claiming we got revolutionary new fountain-of-youth treatments that didn't exist. Delighted everyone by cutting so heavily into the hordes of us who, convinced we had the right to 'retire' back then, were bankrupting social services. Ah, yes, I remember it well." He gazed into the firelight, smiling in apparent wonder.

Catherine smiled, too, touching Philippe's arm. "Grand to remember again, isn't it?" Then she turned back to Mary. "But, with all due respect, dear girl, you were a Boomer. What went wrong?"

They all looked at her, including Brooklyn, who was sanitizing the odd scraps of metal that served as their plates in the flames. Children in the distance were playing "cloned lion," one roaring while chasing the others, who giggled and squealed. Fires dotted the landscape. Depending on the direction of the breeze, Mary could smell either their own or other garbage-dwellers' dinners. Somebody out there had found some rosemary.

Brooklyn squinted at Mary. "'Twas before Boomers' years advanced such that the anti-dementia breakthroughs no longer sufficed, ne?" He hung the plates up in the breeze to cool.

"They still did personality tests!" Philippe said proudly. "*Voilà*, I remember!"

But Brooklyn must have seen what must have been visible on Mary's face and leaped over an upturned old virtual helmet to wrap an arm around her. "Wasup, B?" he whispered gently.

And Mary remembered. She bit her lip against the pain of it. "I...still don't understand how I failed. I tried so hard, over and over and over again."

"Failed the personality tests, dear girl?" Catherine, on the other side of her, asked.

"Yes. And I tried so hard to be sensible and good, and to show them how willing I would be to do exactly as I was told without questioning it ever, no matter what happened. I told them over and over again that I understood that I couldn't do

anything a'tall without the help of others."
Mary watched the others exchange looks.
In the silence that followed Mary listened
to the shish kebobs sizzling.

"Granted," started Catherine, "they
kept this under wraps for decades, but
those Boomer personality tests were
based on the old Mars One criteria dating
back as far as 2012. Didn't you see all
that when it came out later?"

Mary hung her head. Brooklyn
tightened his arm around her. "I...went
through a bad spell," Mary said. "Just
when I finally accepted that my mother had
been right about me, and that I could never
go to the stars, my anti-dementia
treatments started to fail."

"Alas... *C'est la vie, mon chéri*," Philippe said heavily. "Especially because, in the short time I've known you as your real self, it strikes me that you have the exact personality traits they were looking for then."

Mary looked up, startled. "Which were?"

"The capacity for independence and self-reliance." Philippe looked at Brooklyn and Catherine, who nodded when he asked, "*N'est-ce pas?*"

"Then my mother," said Mary, "and her whole world in the south—that I fled as soon as I learned to hitchhike—was completely, absolutely wrong about everything." What irony, what piercing irony. Mary turned, sobbing, to

Brooklyn, striking his shoulder with her fist out of frustration. Finally spent, she wasn't sure she could take it, but she craned her head back to look up at the stars.

Brooklyn kissed her brow, then handed her off to Catherine, who wrapped a much thinner and bonier arm around her.

Mary could hear Brooklyn serving up dinner. But she only had eyes for the stars. "Have you ever wondered," she said to no one in particular, "what it would really be like to be out there?"

She heard the others grunt various acknowledgements through mouthfuls of food. She felt the steam on her chin from a plate her peripheral vision told her had been placed beside her but ignored it.

Mary went on. "The majesty. The serenity. The escape not only from the horror of the southern U.S. in the 1950s but from all the accumulated failings of our kind."

The grunts of acknowledgements were stronger this time.

Brooklyn said, "No cloned lions to disturb our slumber."

Catherine said, "No living amidst the garbage of yet another post-urban disaster."

Philippe said something in French Mary didn't understand, but it sounded like agreement.

Mary looked down, her love for the stars spilling over to these people huddled up in the garbage with her who had suffered as much as she had. Lit by the firelight, their faces glowed as they looked back at her. A wonderful warmth spread over Mary; she wasn't sure whether it came from outside or within. "Independence? Self-reliance? Everything we found with those alligator clips on that purple pug this afternoon? It's not too late. We could find a way. We could all go to the stars!"

"With what money, dear girl?" Catherine asked.

"*De rigueur!*" Philippe added.

"For shame, ye of little faith," said Brooklyn. "No money need be spent amidst such abundance," he continued, waving his hand over the garbage while reaching into his pocket. "But when I presumed to hack into Kane's safe to procure the vials that freed the two of you from being Marilyn Monroe and Napoleon Bonaparte for all eternity, I also availed myself of..." He pulled out a huge wad of money.

SUE HOLLISTER BARR

Jethro no longer cared about himself, figuring with all that he'd done wrong in his life, from racial prejudice to failing to save anyone outside of Vietnam, he wasn't worth it.

But he was determined to succeed just once, no matter what happened to him afterwards.

First, he had to get back out of Boomers for the Stars. Kane being what he was, Jethro had finally, fully accepted that cooperating with his own death wouldn't have any effect on his daughter's safety in the end. But Kane's lust for her should keep her alive till Jethro could get a message to her that would convince her he wasn't paranoid.

Rubber Ducky had been easy. Upside down in the cuddle couch, it timed out from registering all the cuddling as too many typed requests at once. It would probably have to be re-booted, as they used to call it, before it was operational again.

But when he'd tried to exit through the front door, he'd gotten a pretty bad electrical shock. Jethro didn't know where that had come from but figured he better hide in case there was also a silent alarm of some kind associated with this new security measure. And worry about what other fancy new security measures were now in place.

Crouched behind it, Jethro was constantly jostled by the cuddle couch's frenzied attempts to shower Rubber Ducky with adequate comfort and support. He hadn't heard anything: no security door opening, nor the human footsteps he was hoping for so he could get his hands on Kane now that "AAA" was beyond saving. Jethro hadn't even heard the silver bot wheels he dreaded. He'd waited and waited and waited. Time to move on.

Busy reviewing window-exit options while fearing they'd been electrified, too, Jethro barely noticed. Nevertheless, old combat instincts die hard. Something wasn't right, though Jethro couldn't figure out what.

Still behind the couch, he listened again. Silence. What could it be?

Jethro checked what he could see of the dayroom furniture, using a shiny black cabinet that darkly reflected the dayroom on the other side of the cuddle couch. Nothing.

He looked under the couch for feet, wheels, anything. Nothing.

He looked at the faux shag carpet, annoying as always with its constant, unintentional changes of color. He was about to check the only thing left, the ceiling, when something brought his attention back to the carpet, a patch at the end of the couch where he was planning to exit that kept frantically changing from green to purple. He had to squint against the color changes, but wasn't there a slight depression in the carpet? Had he ever seen a depression when there wasn't a—

The depression advanced, just enough for Jethro to identify it as a wheel. He darted around the opposite end of the couch.

The dayroom was empty, silent except for the cuddle couch caressing Rubber Ducky.

Then, ever so slowly and still silently, Jethro saw the carpet depressing for wheels heading toward him from the other end of the couch.

Knowing he was no match for invisible handcuffs, he yanked Rubber Ducky out of the couch, used it as a shield, and backed toward a window.

The wheel depressions picked up speed, heading straight towards him. Jethro struggled to remember both what the now-invisible silver bot looked like and how far in advance of anything the carpet depressed itself.

Rubber Ducky... No glass or wood but at least— Jethro grabbed the rubber part of the bot in his hands and swung it behind him, shattering the window. Mildly conductive, it gave him an electrical shock but not enough to stop him from swinging back around to face the invisible bot just before the wheel depressions reached him.

What Jethro assumed was a handcuff clanged against a non-rubber part of Rubber Ducky. But the other handcuff? Where?

Suddenly he heard something, the faint sound he usually associated with the close proximity of a bot, then, for one brief instant, the silver bot flickered into view without its full-disclosure screen.

Jethro jerked away from where he'd seen the other handcuff coming at him. At the same time he took his best shot at using Rubber Ducky like he'd used his wheelchair to topple Pink Panda long ago, swinging low. Then he bolted out the window.

The weakness in the fence was too far away across open ground. Jethro toyed with darting behind the closest cover and circling around. But, with all these new security measures, would that silver bot be able to track him by something like his body heat? Had it known he was hiding behind the cuddle couch but just been waiting for him to come out for some reason?

Hail Mary... Jethro remembered his days watching football and ran across the open lawn. If he made it, he made it. If he didn't, he didn't. But if he did make it, he was going to save the rest of those organ donors behind the door in that canyon of garbage or die trying.

SUE HOLLISTER BARR

Kane wondered why he still wasn't puking. He'd taken that vial of "Fountain of Youth" Andy had surprised him with hours ago.

He went back to reviewing his to-do list. Especially thanks to the extra features included in Andy's purple-bot homing device, Kane figured he'd gotten through most of the important stuff. Particularly sugoi was the audio/visual component...

Kane smirked. All his missing organ donors together now, planning to go to the stars with his money and Andy's bot? He checked the airpad schedule again to be sure. Yes, the drop in organ prices was impacting everyone, and even the airpad was temporarily cutting back on service. There was only one off-planet launch still scheduled, and that only because it was subsidized by the corporations mining helium-3 on the moon...always in need of more human workers.

His stomach gurgled. The beginning of the nausea? No, just hunger. Kane wondered where Rubber Ducky was with its menu choices. Not to mention the silver security bot...probably off in a corner somewhere, malfunctioning with its full-disclosure screen flickering on and off.

If that silver bot didn't show up soon, Kane would have to go find it and kick it back to life. Only then could he coordinate capturing his missing organ donors and Andy's bot with Mr. Extreme Sports.

His stomach grumbled loudly. Aha! But no, not even a hint of nausea. Kane fished the empty vial out of his pocket.

Hmmm. Kane had assumed that Andy had found an extra vial but maybe not. The vial was unmarked. And Andy had been busy in the lab for a long time just before he gave it to Kane. Sugoi! Must have been that brilliant scientist's last breakthrough, an improvement in the formula.

Kane returned to the screen in front of him. What had he been checking on?

SUE HOLLISTER BARR

SUE HOLLISTER BARR

Mary shimmied without thinking, again trying to rid herself of the salt that kept getting in her nose. But it only made her sneeze more and seemed to fascinate a young man, lugging a full space suit, who paused on his way by.

Mary returned her attention to the window, but she could feel the others gathering around her.

Brooklyn forced her to read a newsfeed story by projecting a screen between her and the view. The breaking story was that Andrew Adams, once considered a prominent scientist, was actually a complete fraud. It turned out all his supposed inventions were mere shams, cribbed from old speculative fiction stories, despite persistent rumors about a fully functional fountain of youth. Legitimate scientists had established that nothing he created worked, and that he had even used an alias, Archibald A. Astor, to try to peddle his snake oil in Africa.

Mary could only hope that wonderful man would be all right with those people in the tall building until she and the others could prove all that wrong.

Brooklyn collapsed the newsfeed screen. Catherine, elegantly cradling the purple pug with one arm like an aristocratic mother, joined Mary on her other side. They each wrapped an arm around her as they pressed against the window on either side of her.

"Dear girl," Catherine said, "this launch we'll soon be on to the moon is only the beginning."

Joining them at the window, Philippe said, "Ooh la la!"

Mary found herself choking strangely. It took her a moment to realize she was both crying and laughing at the same time.

Outside the space elevator's window the last wispy cloud was now gone. The sky was changing from blue to purple. As they watched, so crowded by that space elevator window that Mary could feel them all breathing as one, that oddly purple sky turned to a rich, deep, all-encompassing black.

"One hundred miles high," Brooklyn said.

"*Regardez la Terre!*" exclaimed Philippe, straining to see below them.

But Mary only strained to see above them. And there they were, like she'd never seen them before, blinding, unblinking in all their magnificence.

The stars.

SUE HOLLISTER BARR

Jethro's combat instincts had left him with a perhaps irrational aversion to any confined space he knew he couldn't escape. He fought his claustrophobia by moving around as much as he could, though it hurt a lot. That construction-grade bot had cut deeply into both legs.

It didn't help when some asshole kid bumped into him with a full space suit.

"Whaddaya think this is?" Jethro snapped. "Disneyland? Did you bring your bungee cord?"

The kid looked at him blankly and moved on.

Jethro was about to walk back to check on the canyon organ donors when he finally gave in to the touristy bullshit and looked for a window.

And there they were: Marilyn Monroe, but Jethro could tell from her body language that she wasn't Marilyn Monroe anymore. Napoleon, who seemed taller. Brooklyn, the only one who could have accomplished such a thing, the man who succeeded, thankfully, where Jethro had failed. And Mary...

The last scheduled off-planet launch. Everyone safely connecting from the space elevator for it except for his son and his daughter. He'd railed; he'd screamed. But his children had used every dirty trick in the book to force Jethro to promise to take the canyon organ donors he'd rescued on ahead without them if they couldn't make it in time.

Panting. Jethro could hear it behind him. Then he felt a hand on his shoulder.

It was a light, soft hand. He turned to see his daughter, wreathed in smiles but bathed in sweat and struggling to regain her breath. Behind her, bent over as if he'd just run a race, was his son.

Kane was annoyed. Shimatta!
Suddenly everything seemed so difficult, even
the simplest things.

Like—kuso!—where was his lab bot?
Kane had looked everywhere. But he was
having trouble there, too, getting more and
more confused about where he'd already
looked and where he hadn't yet. Shimatta!
Shimatta! Shimatta! Where was that pink
panda?

And there was something important he
had to remember to do, something about the
moon. Kuso! What was it?

He could only remember that it had
something to do with Pink Panda. Then, it was

355

as if something shifted in his mind. Pink Panda, of course... That stupid bot had to get JFK's kidneys now, while JFK was still alive!

Kane's stomach grumbled, and it occurred to him for a moment that he was ravenously, perhaps clinically, starved.

But then something clicked in his mind again. Yes, of course, he, JFK, was still alive. Why wouldn't he be? And he was going to succeed beyond anyone's wildest dreams by being the first to get a man on the moon. But he had to get busy; he had a speech to deliver. Standing proud, erect, he cleared his throat. "We choose to go to the moon! We choose to go to the moon in this decade..."

OTHER BOOKS BY
SUE HOLLISTER BARR

Craig Healing Springs
Rococo
Ships
Twisted

suehollisterbarr.com